# The Enchanted Antique Shop

CIELLE KENNER

Welcome to Enchanted Springs, where ghosts are friendly, magic is real, and time is anything but linear. This story is a work of fiction. Get maps, character profiles, and free bonus content at ciellekenner.com.

Cover art by The Cover Coven

# Contents

# Chapter 1

G HOSTS HAVE NO SENSE of time.

Don't get me wrong. They understand that time passes. They watch as the seasons change and one year rolls into another. They know that life goes on in this world, and the next.

But what most ghosts don't realize is that living people, the kind with bodies, need to sleep. Apparently, once you slip the surly bonds of earth, you forget that mortals get surly if we don't get a good night's rest.

Which is why I was more than a little testy when Violet Serrano woke me up for the fourth morning in a row. As long as she was around, it would be a challenge for me to rest in peace.

"Hiya, Marley," she said, taking a seat on the edge of my bed, then bouncing up and down as if she was testing my mattress. "The sun's up. Are you planning to come to the shop today?"

I groaned. "Yes. Of course. Don't I come in every day?"

She leaned back to adjust the garters on her stockings, then raised both legs gracefully into the air so she could point her toes and admire her ankles.

To my eyes, Violet didn't look like a ghost. She wasn't faded or transparent. If anything, she had more of a glow than a living person, like an ethereal aura that grew brighter the happier she felt.

Violet had been a free-spirited flapper during the 1920s, and she still favored the look, with a stylish bobbed haircut and a mischievous glint in her eyes. Today she was draped in a shimmering beaded dress with a long string of pearls swinging around her neck.

"Well, Marley, I wanted to make sure. That place is so dead when you're not around."

I pulled a pillow over my face and groaned. The Enchanted Antique Shop might have been filled with ghosts, but they were anything but dead.

She tried to pull the pillow away, but her hand passed through the memory foam and brushed my cheek. I sat up, feeling like she'd thrown cold water on my face. Now her spectral cat Twila was on the bed, too, pawing at a corner of the blanket as if it would unravel the secrets of the universe.

Twila, short for "Twilight," was the ghost of a tiny Siamese kitten. Her fur was a warm beige, with dark brown points on her nose and ears, and her ethereal blue eyes sparkled with an otherworldly light. Like Violet, she was beautiful—but she was also a pest.

I rolled my eyes. I was being haunted, but not by vengeful spirits who wanted me to change my wanton ways. I was being haunted by spirits who wanted me to wake up and entertain them.

I wiped the sleep from my eyes. "Couldn't you at least make coffee?"

"Sorry, toots, no can do. The best I could manage is maybe to push the little button if you get it all set up."

"At that point, I could set the timer myself."

"Yep." She blew a pale pink bubble with her gum, then popped it. "Things are tough all over."

Violet and I were both twenty-nine. Technically, I suppose, Violet was more like a hundred and twenty-nine, but she'd been attached to the antique shop for most of her existence. She was comfortable there, surrounded by vintage treasures that reminded her of her undying youth.

I told her I would come to work soon if she'd leave me alone to shower and get dressed. She bounded to her feet. She scooped the kitten into her arms, grinned, and wiggled her fingers in a brief farewell as her etheric body dissolved into a sparkling constellation of twinkling lights.

---

I hadn't been a shopkeeper for very long. For the last few years, I'd been on an entirely different track, working as a photographer in Miami. I was living the dream—until my life took a sudden and unexpected turn. Without any sort of warning or preparation, I started seeing ghosts and glimpses of living history.

As it turns out, I had entered my astrological Saturn Return, a significant cosmic event that awakened my true powers. The strange occurrences I witnessed weren't random occurrences. Instead, they were manifestations of magic.

I thought I was losing my mind. I hurried home to Enchanted Springs, where I learned I was simply the latest in a line of time-traveling witches. As it turns out, most of the women in my family could see ghosts and peer through the pages of time, including my mother and grandmother. No one told me in advance because those powers were never guaranteed.

As luck would have it, I'd also come into my magic just when the Enchanted Antique Shop needed a new proprietor. It was the perfect place to practice my newfound abilities—especially with my grandmother Clara's bakery, the Enchanted Oven, right across the street.

Now as I drove to the Enchanted Antique Shop, I was struck by the charm of my historic hometown. Even non-magical beings could feel its mystical allure.

Main Street was lined with quirky shops, cozy boutiques, and welcoming cafes. Flags and banners flew from wrought-iron lampposts. Colorful awnings shielded shoppers from the Florida sun, and flowers bloomed in oversized planters. Park benches offered plenty of places to rest along the sidewalk, shaded by green trees and gazebos.

The Enchanted Antique Shop was a landmark that appealed to locals and tourists alike. A vintage sign over the door swayed gently in the breeze, inviting visitors to step inside and explore its hidden treasures. Inside, the shop was a labyrinth of creaking floorboards and narrow aisles. Every nook and cranny was filled with intriguing collectibles.

I walked in and took a deep breath, savoring the delicate scent of aged wood and lemon-scented polish.

The Enchanted Antique Shop was more than just a store; it was a place where history came alive.

My eyes danced from one corner of the shop to the other, taking in the artful displays of vintage jewelry, sparkling glassware, and leather-bound books. Every item had a history, a secret waiting to be discovered, and I reveled in the chance to uncover their mysteries.

Walking through the Enchanted Antique Shop was like walking through a life-sized dollhouse. All three floors had been divided into a series of period displays, thanks to moveable partitions that created room-size vignettes. Customers could stroll through the shop and immerse themselves in the signature style of timeframes from the Victorian era of the 1800s to the atomic age of the 1950s, or saunter from the swinging sixties to the introduction of the Internet in the 1990s.

As I looked around the shop, I couldn't help but smile. Warm, golden sunlight filtered through the windows, casting a magical glow on everything it touched.

An antique mirror caught my eye, its ornate frame glinting in the morning sun. It had been one of my first acquisitions, and it held a special place in my heart. I loved how it reflected all the magic of the shop.

I also caught a glimpse of my own reflection: brown eyes, lopsided grin, and masses of wavy auburn hair pulled back with a headband.

Eleanor Somerville, my mentor, was in her favorite part of the store, a re-creation of an art deco dining room. The walls were adorned with dark red wallpaper featuring geometric patterns in black and silver. She sat in one of four brocade chairs at a table crafted of polished rosewood. A mirrored sideboard displayed a collection of figurines with Egyptian motifs, all inspired by the discovery of King Tut's tomb in 1922.

Eleanor's silver hair gleamed under the soft lighting. She had been the sole proprietor of the Enchanted Antique Shop for more than fifty years. Now semi-retired, she still came in almost every day to help me learn the secrets of the shop—including the complicated mysteries of the storeroom in the back.

Most people in Enchanted Springs didn't realize that our small town was truly enchanted, thanks to a mystic fountain in the center of town. Its dancing water shimmered with an otherworldly glow, and its magic flowed freely, carried on the wind down every street and around every corner.

The Enchanted Antique Shop wasn't merely one of many historic buildings on a picturesque street. Our building was literally *the* most historic structure in town. It was built around an ancient gateway that served as a portal to the past, now conveniently disguised to look like an ordinary storeroom in the back of the shop. As proprietors, Eleanor and I safeguarded its secrets. In the course of our work, we could also travel to other eras and bring important artifacts back to our own time.

Unfortunately, time travel took its toll. After many long years of zipping in and out of history, Eleanor could sometimes lose track of where—and when—she was. It was an occupational hazard I was determined to avoid.

# Chapter 2

THE FRONT OF THE shop featured rotating displays that changed with the seasons. I was arranging a new presentation when I felt a sudden chill. The air seemed to shimmer with a faint, otherworldly glow, which could only mean one thing: Violet was checking in.

"Hey, Marley," she greeted me, her voice like the tinkling of a champagne glass. "I see you pulled that old cowboy hat out of storage."

I smiled as I turned to greet her. "Yep. I thought we should feature it, since the art museum is unveiling Theodore Stevens' portrait tonight."

Theodore Stevens was one of the most famous men ever to live in Enchanted Springs. He was the adventurer who invented the cowboy hat—an icon of American style—and he became a multi-millionaire in the process.

Our local art museum had recently acquired an original portrait of the entrepreneur. It was scheduled to be unveiled at a fundraising gala in his former winter home, the Stevens Mansion. I had been one of the first to buy tickets. I couldn't wait to take a look around the most elegant estate in town.

I stepped back to assess my display, which was still a work in progress. The centerpiece was an original *Boss of the Prairie* hat, with a wide brim and high crown. I'd given it a place of prominence in a plexiglass case to protect it from dust, on a hat stand so visitors could see it from all angles.

Most people who saw the hat would think it was remarkably well preserved. Only a few of us knew Eleanor had traveled back in time to 1872 to buy it.

Violet floated over to the photo of Theodore Stevens I had displayed next to the hat. He looked like a typical turn-of-the-century gentleman: white hair, white beard, stiff white collar, and a suit.

"He sure was a looker, wasn't he?" she sighed.

I chuckled. "He's a little old for my taste, but sure. Did you ever meet him?"

"Once or twice, in passing." Violet sighed and shook her head. "But not while we were alive. We met a few years after he died. Now that he's a ghost, I guess he spends most of his time up in his old hat factory in Pittsburgh."

I was about to photograph the Stevens display for social media when the shop bell rang, and a man in a ten-gallon hat walked through the door. As he stepped inside, I was struck by his imposing height and his cowboy swagger. He was well over six feet tall, with broad shoulders and a chiseled jaw. Based on his leathery, sun-lined face, I guessed he was in his mid- to late sixties. His piercing blue eyes scanned the room, framed by thick, dark eyebrows that seemed to dance with every expression. He wore a western-style shirt, well-worn Levis, and a pair of polished cowboy boots.

He tipped his hat in my direction. "Well, howdy, miss."

Then he took a few steps closer to the display I was arranging. "Is that an authentic *Boss of the Prairie*?"

I nodded. "It's one of the first hats Theodore Stevens produced. We think it dates back to 1872."

"Name your price."

I turned to him and smiled. "I would, but we haven't had it appraised yet."

He bent down to look more closely at the hat. "Ma'am, my name is Julian Wainwright, and I reckon I'm as much of an expert as you'll find when it comes to Theodore Stevens. An original *Boss of the Prairie* hat, in what seems to be mint condition, would fetch upwards of five million dollars at one of them fancy European auctions."

"Are you offering me five million?"

He laughed. "Well, I'd have to get it appraised, of course."

He studied the hat further, a far-away look on his face. "Where did you get it?"

"Believe it or not, it was in the storeroom here at the shop. I only recently took over, so I found it while I was going through our inventory."

He raised an eyebrow, as if he didn't quite believe me. I kept talking anyway.

"I agree that it's in beautiful condition," I said. "Given the importance of Theodore Stevens to this community, I think it's possible that we'll decide to keep it as a display piece."

He nodded agreeably. "That makes sense. I just flew in from Texas to see his mansion and get a glimpse of that new painting they're unveiling."

"Then let me welcome you to Enchanted Springs. My name is Marley Montgomery. Where are you from in Texas?"

"Well, I got me a little ranch of about two hundred thousand acres in Hill Country, a few hours outside of Dallas."

I made a small adjustment to the plexiglass case and brushed my hands on my sides. "I'll be at the gala myself. Here in Enchanted Springs, it's pretty much the social event of the season."

He chuckled. "It's one of the highlights of my season, too."

"We have a few other old Theodore Stevens collectibles over here, if you're interested."

I led him to a display case that held an assortment of trinkets and keepsakes. A gold pocket watch caught his attention.

"The case features an engraving of the Stevens hat factory," I explained, handing it to him. "It's also engraved with a retirement thank-you note to one of his employees."

Julian's eyes lit up with enthusiasm. "This will make a splendid addition to my collection." He looked at the price tag. "And the price is far less than five million dollars."

At the checkout desk, as he reached for his wallet, the movement of his arm opened his suit jacket to reveal a walnut-handled pistol in a holster at his side.

Violet floated over beside him, her eyes fixated on the gun. "That's a vintage Peacemaker," she said, her voice tinged with excitement. "A Colt .45. My husband used to carry one just like it! I haven't seen one of those in years."

I tried to play it cool. Not because of the pistol, but because of Violet. After all, Enchanted Springs was a small town in a rural setting, with plenty of farmers and ranchers who carried firearms.

Most people, however, had no idea that Enchanted Springs was also populated with ghosts, spirits, and people of the paranormal persuasion. When ordinary visitors stopped in, I didn't want them to see me talking to my invisible friends.

Violet tried to pull his jacket back to get a closer look at the pistol, but her ghostly hand passed right through the fabric. Julian Wainwright looked around as if he'd felt a cool breeze, then shrugged and handed me a credit card.

# Chapter 3

I LEFT THE SHOP that afternoon just as our cleaning woman arrived. Hazel Turner owned Turnkey Cleaning, and she kept the store spotless. With her gentle smile and meticulous attention to detail, she helped ensure that every corner of the shop was bright and inviting.

We exchanged friendly greetings, and then she went about her work, dusting shelves and mopping floors.

With my parents away on sabbatical, I'd been staying in our family home—which we sometimes laughingly referred to as "Montgomery Manor." It was old farmhouse with high ceilings, big windows, and a welcoming front porch. When it was built, the house was on the outskirts of Enchanted Falls. As the town grew, the house did, too, with the addition of a large living room, comfortable eat-in kitchen, and a den for my stepfather. All the rooms were filled with vintage furnishings and heirlooms passed down through generations of the Montgomery family.

I climbed the creaking staircase to my bedroom on the second floor. Soft, natural light filtered through lace curtains. An old brass bed filled one side of the room, offset by a sitting area with two armchairs and an ottoman. The furniture was mismatched, but somehow it all fit together like a patchwork quilt. A paneled door led to a bathroom with a clawfoot tub, along with a small dressing area with a vanity and full-length mirror.

I always struggle with dressing for formal events. At 5'2", I'm definitely on the short side, which means it's easy for me to look like a little girl playing dress-up. But for the fundraising gala at the Stevens Mansion, I was determined to find something that would make me feel elegant and alluring.

After trying on what felt like a dozen different vintage dresses in the shop, I had settled on a little black cocktail dress from the 1950s. The color suited my complexion, and the fitted bodice and flouncy skirt flattered my figure. The neckline was modest but still showed a hint of skin, and the beading added just the right amount of sparkle. To add a touch of glamor, I paired the dress with strappy silver heels and chandelier earrings that brushed my shoulders. I even tried a fancy updo with my long curls, sweeping my hair to the side and securing it with a sparkly comb. It wasn't perfect, but it would do.

When I looked in the mirror, I laughed with delight. I looked like an adult—or, as my grandmother would say, a fancy grown-up lady. I was ready for a sophisticated soiree in a marvelous mansion.

First, though, I needed to pick up my witch friend Sadie. By day, she was a history professor at Magnolia University. By night, she was an old-school spellcaster.

Sadie could weave intricate and potent charms, imbuing ordinary objects with extraordinary qualities. She could cast spells of protection, luck, and even subtle persuasion. But she was a historian, first and foremost, so she infused her charms and enchantments with ancient symbols, incantations, and forgotten magical practices. Every talisman she forged carried a whisper of the past, weaving the tapestry of time with the hidden forces that shaped the world.

Sadie had been looking forward to seeing the old Stevens Mansion for weeks. I pulled up in front of her house and she hopped into my Volkswagen convertible, her eyes sparkling with excitement. She wore a fitted sleeveless dress with a simple strand of pearls. Her platinum hair was cut into a chic French bob with blunt bangs, and tonight she had styled it with glamorous finger waves. Her makeup was on point, too, with matte red lipstick, dark arched brows, and a swoosh of black eyeliner.

We drove to the mansion, beneath a glowing full moon that lit our way. The streets of Enchanted Springs were lined with quaint cottages and bungalows, each one unique and welcoming in its own way. Towering water oaks spun with Spanish moss created a canopy overhead, while night-blooming jasmine scented the air.

The wrought-iron gates of the Stevens Mansion opened automatically as we approached. Strings of twinkling fairy lights cast a warm glow over the well-manicured grass, and a valet was waiting to park our car.

As we walked up a stone pathway to the door, I couldn't help but admire the flower beds surrounding the house. They looked like formal gardens on a castle estate, and I felt like we had stepped into a mystical, dreamlike world.

Sadie had researched the mansion before we came. "This place cost a small fortune to build back in the 1880s," she said. "If you could even find the specialized craftsmen you would need to build it today, it would probably cost ten or twenty million to re-create."

As we reached the grand entrance, the sound of laughter and chatter grew louder. We rang, and the heavy wooden doors swung open. A butler greeted us, dressed in a crisp black tuxedo with a white shirt and black bow tie. He checked our tickets, bowed, and stepped aside, inviting us in with a graceful sweep of his hand.

Abigail Foster, the Wards' estate manager, came into view. She was a tall, slender woman in her late forties, with emerald eyes and a welcoming smile that highlighted her cleft chin. She wore an elegant navy dress, pearl earrings, and a vintage brooch engraved with patterned leaves. Her strawberry blonde hair was twisted into an elegant chignon at the nape of her neck.

"Welcome, Marley!" Abigail said, her voice friendly and genuine. "This must be your friend Sadie, the history professor?"

"Yes, of course. Sadie, meet Abigail. She manages the mansion for the Wards."

The two women exchanged warm greetings. Abigail smiled as she continued. "Wait until you see how perfect the antique lamp you sold me looks in the drawing room. It's the ideal accent piece for the space."

Abigail was a frequent visitor at the shop. She stopped in regularly in search of collectables to add to the mansion's decor. We had developed a friendly rapport, and I always appreciated her keen eye for quality and her knowledge of antiques.

Sadie and I walked through the opulent foyer, while Abigail continued to greet guests at the door. As we stepped further into the house, we gazed in wonder at the grand staircase, the polished marble floors, and the glittering chandeliers.

Sadie leaned in and whispered, "There's so much history here! I could spend hours exploring this place."

We continued to take in the sights and sounds as we made our way into the ballroom, where the gala was underway. The chatter and laughter of the attendees filled the air, creating an atmosphere of excitement and anticipation. A string quartet played classical music near the fireplace, and uniformed servers passed drinks and hors d'oeuvres on silver platters.

The ballroom had been transformed into a feast for the senses, with several buffet stations set up around the room. The first station featured an array of fresh fruit, including plump strawberries, juicy watermelon, and succulent grapes. The second boasted an impressive display of artisanal cheese and crackers. The third station was filled with iced platters of succulent seafood, including chilled shrimp cocktail and oysters on the half shell. Next up was the carving station, where a massive slab of roast beef was being expertly sliced by a chef in a white toque. Finally, the dessert station offered an impressive selection of bite-size sweets, all artfully arranged on platters and stands. I smiled when I saw how beautiful it looked, because my grandmother Clara had catered that portion of the buffet. I snapped a few photos with my cell phone so she could showcase it later.

The true centerpiece of the evening, however, was the museum's new portrait, currently standing on an ornamental easel and bathed in a soft spotlight. At the moment, the portrait remained veiled, its secrets shrouded beneath a red velvet drape. The heavy borders of the framed canvas seemed to glow with an air of anticipation, as if the artwork itself was holding its breath before its dramatic introduction.

In the buildup to the gala, we'd heard all about the history of the painting, but the image on the canvas had been kept a closely guarded secret. I couldn't wait to see it for myself.

# Chapter 4

I FOUND MYSELF IN the middle of the crowd as Quinn Delaney, the museum director, stepped up to the microphone to address the guests.

Quinn was slender, with golden blonde hair cut into a fashionable pixie style. She was from London, and her speech carried a distinctive British accent.

"Ladies and gentlemen, thank you ever so much for joining us. Tonight promises to be a most memorable evening. We are so thrilled to unveil our newest acquisition for the Enchanted Springs Museum of Art. I know for a fact that when you see it, you'll be delighted, too. It's a remarkable work, a life-size portrait of Theodore Stevens, painted by the acclaimed eighteenth-century artist James Sinclair Sterling."

I accepted a glass of champagne from a waiter as he passed by. The aroma was heady, with hints of fresh fruit. The bubbles burst on my tongue, sweet and succulent, and I'm not ashamed to admit I drank it all in just a few sips. When the waiter walked by again, I reached for another.

Quinn continued speaking. "We do so appreciate all of your contributions to tonight's fundraiser. I'm pleased to inform you that your donations have exceeded our goal—but that doesn't mean we would refuse additional contributions." With a playful smile, she elicited a moment of bemused laughter from the crowd.

"Of course, we couldn't have held our gala tonight without the support and generosity of our smashing hosts, Gregory and Hillary Ward." Quinn gestured to a couple standing nearby, encouraging them to come to the microphone.

Hillary, dressed in a flamboyant orange gown, offered a queenly wave to the crowd. Gregory tried to act suave and sophisticated, but he stepped on the cuff of his tuxedo pants and stumbled as he approached. Hillary's bleached-blonde hair was teased into an expansive bouffant. Her husband had stretched a long, well-oiled comb-over across the top of his head, spanning the vast expanse of his shiny pate from one ear to the other.

Gregory sniffed loudly and swallowed something. He hunched forward to talk into the microphone, his voice several decibels louder than necessary. "What an amazing night it is! We hope you all enjoy the fantastic painting and the wonderful atmosphere of our picture-perfect home."

Hillary took the microphone off the stand, and after a burst of high-pitched feedback, she curled her top lip back in what probably passed for a smile. "Tonight is a rare night, in which we open our doors to you, the common people of Enchanted Springs, so that you may experience firsthand the luxury and sophistication of a home far beyond your means."

Sadie and I looked at each other in surprised amusement. Granted, the Stevens Mansion was the only home of its kind in town, but our hostess was talking to us as if we were peasants.

Hillary handed the microphone back to Quinn. Then she and her husband pressed their hands together in front of their chests, prayer style, and bowed in unison.

Quinn raised her eyebrows slightly, then took a deep breath and resumed speaking. "Ladies and gentlemen, we have a special guest with us tonight, here to share some insight into the remarkable artist who created this masterpiece. Please welcome Calvin Carter, an art historian who has traveled all the way from Orlando to be with us."

A ruddy-looking man in his forties took the stage. He had a shaggy fringe of fiery red hair and a matching red goatee. He scanned the audience, his eyes wide and bulging.

"Thank you, Quinn," he began, his voice shaking with nervous tension. He pulled an index card from his jacket pocket and began to read in a stilted monotone.

"Artist James Sinclair Sterling, 1850 to 1918, was considered the leading portrait painter of his generation. He had a distinctive style, characterized by a luminous, dreamlike palette, enhanced by his stumbling technique."

I knew from high school art classes that scumbling was a way to soften colors with a dry paintbrush. This speaker, however, used "stumbling," instead, as if the painter was tripping and falling all over the canvas. I chalked his error up to nerves.

Calvin paused for a moment and looked around uncertainly. He licked his lips, then returned to the notecard in his hand. His voice was louder now, but still monotonous. One sentence ran into another as he raced to get through his prepared comments. "As an artist, James Sinclair Sterling was a master of capturing the human form and his use of light and shadow to create three-dimensional effects was revolutionary for his time. He had a unique ability to create portraits that looked extremely lifelike. His signature style included an effect that made it seem as if the eyes of his subjects were following viewers around the room, which added a sense of intimacy and connection to his pieces."

Then he stopped talking. I couldn't tell if he was done with his remarks or if he had lost his place. He swallowed nervously and looked over at the museum director. "That's all I wrote down," he said.

The audience offered a smattering of applause as he stepped away from the microphone.

At a nod from Quinn, the string quartet played a thrilling fanfare. It was time to unveil the portrait. Gregory and Hillary stood on either side of the painting, with their hands clasped around the tasseled cords that would reveal the work. We all took a deep breath as the music swelled into a dramatic and awe-inspiring crescendo.

As the velvet cloth dropped, a collective gasp escaped from the crowd.

# Chapter 5

THE PAINTING WAS MORE than lifelike. Once the red drape had fallen to the floor, it seemed as though Theodore Stevens was standing before us in full, living color. I had to blink once or twice to convince myself that I was looking at a painting and not a costumed re-enactor.

I leaned over toward Sadie, brushing up against her side. "Are you seeing what I'm seeing?"

She exhaled. "Wow. That portrait was painted right here, in this room!"

In fact, the painting itself had been positioned in the same spot that Theodore Stevens had been standing when he posed for the portrait. The backdrop of the painting was the marble fireplace where a fire blazed at this very moment. The artist had captured the dazzling crystal chandelier that hung over our heads, still casting a soft glow across the room. He had painted the same gilded mirror that hung over the fireplace, creating a picture-in-a-picture effect that reflected the beauty that surrounded us. And now, because we were all in the same space we saw in the painting, it felt like Theodore Stevens himself was standing in the room with us.

Theodore Stevens had been a handsome man, just as Violet had said. His white hair was wavy and thick, parted to one side and swept back from his forehead. His mustache and beard were white, too, and he wore a suit with a waistcoat and tie. In his left hand he held one of his iconic Stevens hats, just like the one in my antique shop.

Gasps of admiration and applause filled the room. As the crowd quieted, the museum director stepped up to the microphone and beamed. "Now you see why we wanted to unveil the portrait here in the Stevens Mansion," she said.

Gregory Ward stepped between Quinn and the microphone. He grinned like a Cheshire cat and held up his hands as if he was urging the crowd to quell their cheering, even though the applause had already died down.

He cleared his throat, a phlegmy sound that was magnified by the microphone. "Ahem. Hem, hem, ahem." It almost sounded like he was gargling. He gulped and swallowed whatever mucus he had generated in the process. Sadie elbowed me and whispered under her breath so only I could hear her. "Ew. Gross." I bit my tongue, trying not to laugh.

Gregory made one final rattling noise before he spoke. "My wife Hillary and I knew it was both our honor and our civic duty to make the Stevens Mansion available for this event," he announced. He reached out his hand and pulled his wife closer to him. She was beaming, her blindingly white veneers glinting under the spotlight aimed at the microphone.

"As you know, Hillary and I have done far more than our share in renovating and refurbishing this grand home, and we are proud to open our doors occasionally to give the rest of you a glimpse of its glamor and allure."

The crowd applauded feebly. Before he could go on, I noticed Quinn nodding toward the string quartet. The musicians resumed their performance, and Gregory Ward stepped reluctantly away from the spotlight.

It felt almost surreal to stand there in the grand ballroom, seeing the room in real life while simultaneously noticing every detail represented on canvas, too. As I sipped my champagne and gazed at the portrait, Sadie stepped away to say hello to some of her colleagues from Magnolia University.

That's when I noticed Julian Wainwright making his way toward me. He was already the tallest man in the room, and given his signature Stevens cowboy hat, he was impossible to miss.

He grinned as he approached, pulling his newly acquired gold watch from his vest pocket. "Howdy, Miss Marley. I have to show you how good this here timepiece looks, now that one of the jewelers in town done added a gold chain so I could wear it tonight. I'm telling you, this here ol' pocket watch is finer than frog hair."

Once again, I admired the intricate design of the timepiece. "It's beautiful," I agreed.

Julian turned toward the painting. "Well, this portrait is a right sure masterpiece. That Mr. Theodore Stevens looks like he could step right out of the frame and talk with us, doesn't he?"

I followed his gaze to the portrait, and my heart skipped a beat as the famous hatmaker in the painting seemed to turn his head and look at me.

"You're not kidding," I replied, trying to sound nonchalant. "It almost looks like he's alive."

Julian slipped his watch back into his vest. "I surely do wish I could have met him in person." He chuckled. "Of course, you'd have to be a time traveler to make that happen."

At that moment, I could have sworn the man in the painting turned back toward the Texan. Normally, when ghosts approached or I saw time shift, the air shimmered and I felt a vibrating sensation. The artwork, however, didn't have any of the hallmarks I was used to seeing in supernatural situations.

I shook my head, wondering if I'd had too much champagne. When I looked at the portrait again, Theodore Stevens was once again facing forward, his painted form unmoving.

At that point, I noticed my grandmother Clara over near the dessert table. She scanned the rows of tiny lemon tarts, chocolate eclairs, and cream puffs arranged on silver platters. Each confection looked more tempting than the last. Her cupcakes were iced to perfection, adorned with tiny edible sugar flowers. Macarons in every color of the rainbow were stacked in a perfect pyramid, looking almost too pretty to eat. Bite-size cookies and brownies rounded out the array.

She straightened one of the trays, and then she made her way over toward me. I introduced her to the Texan at my side.

"Gram, this is Julian Wainwright. He's a rancher from Texas who also happens to collect Theodore Stevens memorabilia. He came by the shop yesterday and picked up the pocket watch."

Julian beamed at my grandmother, and I wondered for a moment if he was interested in her. While she was in her seventies, she had the figure of a woman half her age. Her laugh lines accentuated the twinkle in her eyes, and her bright smile revealed a matched set of dimples.

Julian pulled the watch from his pocket, happy to show it off again. "Got it all gussied up, too."

"It's a lovely piece," Gram said. "It suits you."

As he tucked the watch away, I think he blushed.

"What do you think of the painting?" Gram asked, nodding toward the life-sized portrait.

Julian turned to face it. "I've been an admirer of Theodore Stevens my whole life. I'd say this piece is a splendid tribute to an admirable gentleman."

She stepped forward to take a closer look. "Theodore Stevens was a great man. He built schools for the children of his factory workers up in Pittsburgh. He also helped fund our own Magnolia University here in Enchanted Springs. I remember hearing stories about him when I was a little girl."

She looked back at Julian, her eyes twinkling. "Now, speaking of history, have you tried the key lime tarts? I made them from a recipe that's been in our family for generations."

"I haven't yet."

"Well, then, we must rectify that situation. Come with me," she said, taking his arm and leading him to the dessert table.

As the evening wound down and guests trickled away, Sadie and I stayed behind to help Gram with the cleanup. We found our way to the kitchen, where Gram was working alongside her colleague, Sylvia Robinson.

A transplant from southern Georgia, Sylvia was the owner of Southern Comfort Catering. She and Gram often worked together at big events. Their ersatz partnership meant Sylvia could focus on main dishes and sides, while Gram handled baked goods and desserts.

Sylvia's long, dark hair was braided, pulled into a high ponytail, and accented with a multicolored scarf that framed her face.

She greeted us warmly, a smile spreading across her face as we entered. "Well, y'all are just the sweetest things for offerin' to help," she drawled, wiping her hands on her apron. "It's always a bit of a scramble to pack up after an event like this."

Sylvia and my grandmother moved about the kitchen with practiced ease, working quickly and efficiently to gather their equipment. One of Sylvia's assistants washed dishes and stacked them in crates, while Sadie wiped the counters and I swept the floor. With several of us working, it took almost no time to load everyone's gear into the catering vans outside.

Finally, the kitchen was spotless, and the catering teams were ready to leave. Grandma Clara thanked us for the help, and Sylvia hugged us both. "If your granny ever disrespects you," she said, eyes twinkling, "y'all can join my crew anytime."

Sylvia glanced at her watch and made her way to the hosts. Gregory and Hillary Ward were standing in the ballroom with a small group of guests, laughing and sipping from champagne flutes and tumblers of whisky.

Sylvia softly cleared her throat and motioned for Gregory to join her a few steps away.

"Mr. Ward, I wanted to let you know the kitchen is all cleaned up, and we've packed our equipment into the van," Sylvia said, her tone professional.

"That's great, Sylvia. Thank you for all your hard work tonight. We'll have Abigail mail you a check."

I glanced around the room. Abigail was nowhere to be seen.

Sylvia raised her eyebrows and glared at Gregory Ward. "Oh, no, sir. That will not do. We agreed on full payment upon completion of the evening."

Hillary turned her head toward the two of them and scowled. Her voice sounded shrill and unnecessarily loud. "We heard you, Miss Sylvia, and Mr. Ward was quite clear. Our assistant will put your check in the mail tomorrow."

Sylvia's expression hardened. "We had an agreement, Mr. Ward."

Gregory stiffened and turned away, rejoining his guests. "Sylvia, we appreciate your contribution tonight, but you know how it is in business. Checks come when they come."

Sylvia shook her head, her voice firm. "That's not how it is in *my* business. I'll give y'all until tomorrow mornin', but I will be back, and I do expect to be paid in full when I get here."

The Wards turned their backs on her. As Sylvia walked away, Hillary whispered under her breath. "What an *uppity* woman." Everyone heard the slur. Sylvia stormed out of the ballroom, holding her head high.

Sadie looked upset. "That's not good," she said.

"No, it's not," Grandma Clara agreed. "If I didn't know better, I'd suspect the Wards are trying to pull a fast one on her."

# Chapter 6

THAT NIGHT, I TOSSED and turned in bed. No matter how I tried, I couldn't get comfortable. As I lay there, staring up at the ceiling, a flicker of movement caught my eye. I turned to see Twila, the ghost cat, sitting on my nightstand and watching me intently.

"Twila, what are you doing here?" I was surprised, but not entirely alarmed. I was getting used to the spectral kitten's antics by now.

Twila leaped from the nightstand to my bed and curled up against me, her tiny body warm against mine. Normally, any physical contact with ghosts feels creepy and cold, but ghost pets are the exception to the rule. I stroked her fur absentmindedly. My mind still raced with thoughts of the gala and the strange interaction Sylvia had experienced with the Wards.

As I drifted off to sleep, however, I could have sworn I sensed Twila projecting her thoughts into my mind. "Secrets, secrets, secrets," she purred.

I was too tired to wonder what she meant. I closed my eyes and fell into a fitful, restless sleep, filled with dark shadows and disturbing dreams.

I dreamed I was in the Stevens Mansion again, but now it was empty. There was no sign of life. Twila materialized, and together we wandered through vacant corridors, into empty rooms, one after another, until we reached the attic. There, positioned in the center of an old farmhouse table, I saw Julian's gold pocket watch. It was ticking loudly, and when I reached for it, it exploded like a bomb.

I woke up, and the dark night sky had given way to the rosy glow of dawn.

Try as I might, I couldn't get back to sleep. Soft light was streaming through my lace curtains, and Twila was nowhere to be found.

I showered, got dressed, and made my bed. I must have been tossing and turning more than I realized. I straightened the quilt, plumped the pillows, and admired the brass bed frame, with its elegant curves and intricate details.

When I noticed my camera bag on my dresser, I reluctantly decided to leave it at home for the day. I couldn't justify toting it along if I didn't have a specific assignment in mind. My cell phone was enough for snapshots and social media, and I didn't have any plans to do more professional photography anytime soon. Maybe someday I would get back to it.

I headed downtown to get an early start on my day. After a quick stop at Black's Coffee Shop for a morning brew, I made my way to the Enchanted Antique Shop.

From the outside, I noticed how trim and neat it looked, especially given its age. The windows were sparkling clean, and the brickwork was in pristine condition.

As soon as I unlocked the front door, Violet materialized. Her form was hazy at first, like a mirage, but gradually her shape became more defined. She wore a simple drop-waist dress with short, ruffled sleeves. The fabric shimmered in the light as if it were made of gossamer.

She was standing so close to me that I had to take a step back or risk walking right through her. She took a step forward, crowding me even more.

"About time, dollface," she said, her hands on her hips. "What the heck happened at that shindig last night?"

"Oh, it was nice," I replied, skirting my way around her. I didn't want to bump into her ethereal body, but she wasn't giving me much room to walk. "Gram's desserts were amazing, and the new portrait of Theodore Stevens was astounding."

"Yeah, yeah, yeah, I'm sure. But what else happened?" She was chewing ghostly gum again, and she snapped it impatiently.

"I don't know. There were some speeches, I guess, and a string quartet played music."

"Don't be such a silly goose. I'm talking about the big event."

I stood still. She was standing uncomfortably close, and I felt her energy pulsing around me like a magnetic field.

"You mean the unveiling of the portrait?"

She shook her head in frustration. "No, poppet, I'm talking about the birdie in the back room. Word in the spirit world is that we've got a new resident on our side of the veil, all because of something that happened at your soiree last night."

I felt a chill run down my spine. I had a bad feeling about this.

"Are you saying there's been a death at the Stevens Mansion?"

"I don't know the details," Violet admitted. "I'd go over there myself, but there's another ghost on the property I've been trying to avoid."

"What? Who?"

"Oh, just someone I used to know. That's not important right now." Her head tilted to one side, and she shrugged her slender shoulders. "You know how it is."

I didn't, but I'd have to ask her about it later.

I shrugged my purse over my shoulder and turned toward the door. "I still have an hour before the shop opens," I said. "I'll head over and see what's going on."

# Chapter 7

I N THE EARLY MORNING hours, Enchanted Springs was normally quiet. Today it was even more placid than usual. Most businesses weren't open yet, so only a few people walked along the sidewalks, carrying coffee cups or walking their dogs.

My friend Ivy Sheridan owned the old bank building, which she used as the headquarters of her real-estate firm. As I passed, I saw the ghost of a former bank manager heading up the steps. He wore a pinstriped suit and carried a heavy leather briefcase. He nodded to me as I drove by, and I smiled back at him.

Further down the street, I saw the ghost of Mrs. Miller, who had been the town's elderly librarian back when I was a child. She was sitting on a bench outside the library, surrounded by a stack of spectral library books. As I drove past, she looked up and waved, her spectacles perched on the end of her nose.

The Stevens Mansion looked different in the light of day. The imposing Victorian loomed over the flowerbeds, casting them in shadow. As I approached the front door, I felt like it was blocking me from the sunlight, too, as if it wanted to whisper tales from a dark and distant past.

During the party, the atmosphere had been festive and alive. Now it seemed as if a pall had been cast over the stately home. The only movement I saw was the gentle sway of curtains in an upstairs window.

I felt like an intruder, an unwelcome trespasser on an unwanted mission. Then I noticed that the front door was standing partially open. Something felt wrong, but I couldn't quite put my finger on it.

I stepped onto the front porch, calling out, "Hello? Is anybody here?"

My heart quickened with a sense of dread.

Pushing open the massive wooden door, I felt the hinges groan, as if the house was protesting my intrusion. The dimly lit foyer revealed itself, adorned with antique furniture and paintings of scenes from Central Florida. Dust motes danced in the rays of morning sun, casting an eerie glow on the room.

Then I saw Sylvia standing at the bottom of the spiraling grand staircase, yelling up the steps. Her hands were on her hips, and her back was to me. "Gregory Ward! Hillary Ward! I am here for my money, and I don't appreciate being ignored. Y'all better come on down with a check in your hand."

The air was thick with anger, and I felt like I was in the middle of a brewing storm. Maybe this confrontation is what Violet had warned me about.

"Sylvia," I asked, as gently as I could. "What's going on? Are you okay?"

Sylvia turned to face me, her eyes fiery with indignation. "Oh, I'm just dandy! Who doesn't like being ghosted when money is due?"

"Do you think they're ignoring you?"

She snorted, her anger not diminishing in the slightest. "Oh, I'm sure of it!"

"How did you get in?"

She paused, considering. "Now that you ask, it was the strangest thing. When I got here, the door was wide open. They must have seen me coming and vamoosed."

At that moment, Quinn Delaney arrived. She stepped through the still-open door and into the foyer where we stood. Her face was etched with concern as she addressed us.

"What do you mean, the door was open? Where are the Wards?"

A look of sheer panic washed over her face as she realized the implications. "Oh, my heavens, the painting!"

She rushed toward the ballroom. Sylvia and I exchanged wary glances as we followed, our footsteps echoing through the empty corridors. The beautiful home seemed to be void of life. There were no lights, no sounds of movement, no signs of anyone within these walls.

As we raced through the elegantly appointed mansion, I couldn't shake the feeling that something was terribly wrong. It was as if the house itself was holding its breath, waiting for us to discover its darkest secrets.

Finally, we reached the grand ballroom, still staged with tables and chairs from the night before. My heart skipped a beat when I saw the display easel in the center of the room.

The painting was gone.

Quinn gasped in shock and seemed frozen in fear, staring at the space where the priceless artwork had been unveiled.

"Where is it?" she whispered, her voice trembling. "Who could have taken it? What could have happened to the painting?"

Sylvia looked around the room, her eyes darting from one corner to another. "It's gone, sugar." She shook her head in disbelief. "Lord, have mercy, someone done stole your art piece."

My mind raced, trying to put the puzzle together. The absent homeowners, the open door, and now the missing portrait. The three peculiarities felt interconnected, and my paranormal instincts were tingling on high alert.

I placed a reassuring hand on Quinn's shoulder, looking into her fearful eyes. "Don't worry, Quinn. We'll find your painting."

I pulled out my phone and dialed the number for the local police. My heart pounded in my chest as the call connected and I relayed the details of the situation.

Within minutes, Jack Edgewood arrived on the scene.

Tall, dark, and handsome, he had been one of the first immortals I'd met when I came into my powers and moved back to Enchanted Springs. It wasn't just his timeless good looks that intrigued me. It was his backstory.

Jack was more than a police detective: he was an ageless vampire. He was powerful enough to endure sunlight, but still human enough to care about truth and justice.

Jack had always caught my eye. I couldn't deny feeling a spark of attraction, but he had never once looked at me with anything but polite disinterest.

Jack took off his fedora and aviator sunglasses and looked around the grand ballroom, squinting as his eyes adjusted to the light. He took in every detail at a glance.

"Marley," he said, his voice calm and collected, "tell me what you know."

I filled him in on the absent mansion owners, the unpaid catering bill, and the missing painting. As I spoke, I could see the gears turning in his mind, piecing the puzzle together.

Once I finished, he nodded thoughtfully. "We need to search the mansion, top to bottom. I'll have my team join us."

Sylvia and Quinn looked relieved, grateful for the reinforcements.

As we waited for more police to arrive, I couldn't help but steal an occasional glance at Jack. I'd seen him many times since I moved back home. He was a frequent visitor in my grandmother Clara's bakery. Sometimes he was there when I dashed in for an occasional pick-me-up, and sometimes I saw him when I looked out the window from my shop. Apparently cops really do like doughnuts.

He wasn't nearly as fond of antiques, though, because he'd only come into my place once since I'd moved back to town.

As soon as Jack's team arrived, the atmosphere shifted dramatically. Officers swarmed the mansion, their voices a cacophony of questions and directives. They examined the empty easel, surveyed the grand ballroom, and spread out through the mansion and across the estate. A moment earlier, the house had been silent. Now it was filled with shouts and footsteps from the hustle and bustle of the investigation.

Quinn, her voice frantic, kept explaining the importance of the missing painting. "It's priceless! I knew I shouldn't have left it here, but Gregory and Hillary insisted it would be safe." She was seething. "I knew I couldn't trust them."

Sylvia, now even more livid, stomped around the room, her southern drawl becoming more pronounced as she vented to anyone who would listen. "I don't have time for any of this nonsense. Ain't nobody got time for this."

Amid the commotion, four men stomped in, wearing matching t-shirts from a party rental place. They were unfazed by the swarm of police officers. Without a moment's hesitation, they started slamming the folding chairs closed and collapsing the tables, oblivious to the surrounding chaos.

As they clattered and banged away, Jack whistled to get their attention. "Hey, guys! This is an active police investigation. You'll have to come back later."

The four men paused, finally registering their surroundings. They exchanged confused glances before nodding and leaving the ballroom.

Officers moved in every direction. The tension in the room mounted. Jack delegated tasks, directed his team, and managed the chaos with an air of authority. As he caught my eye, he motioned for me to step aside with him.

"Marley," he said, his voice firm yet gentle, "I appreciate your help, but it's best if you head back to your shop. We'll handle things here."

Though I understood his reasoning, I couldn't help but feel a twinge of disappointment. Reluctantly, I agreed to leave. I could only hope that the truth would be revealed, and the priceless painting would be found.

Just as Jack was telling me to leave, however, I felt a shiver run down my spine. I recognized the sensation. A ghostly visitor was about to make his presence known.

# Chapter 8

As I stood there, waiting to see who would appear, Theodore Stevens flickered into view. His apparition flickered like a mirage as his spirit wavered between two worlds. He blinked in and out, alternating between transparency and a more solid, albeit ghostly, appearance. It was as if he was struggling to maintain his connection with the physical world. The spirits in my shop could manifest at will, but Theodore wavered in his entrance as if he were out of practice.

I glanced around to see if anyone else had noticed the spectral figure, but only I could see him. Jack, still caught up in the chaos of the investigation, hadn't noticed that I wasn't going anywhere.

Taking a deep breath, I turned to Jack, the words tumbling out of me. "Jack, I can't leave. Theodore Stevens is here."

I saw the surprise in Jack's eyes as he processed my words, but he seemed willing to entertain the possibility. After all, he knew about the unique abilities that ran in my family.

As the ghostly figure of Theodore Stevens solidified, he looked exactly as he did in the painting.

His attire was the epitome of Victorian fashion. He wore a dark three-piece suit, complete with a pocket watch chain draped across his waistcoat. His crisp white shirt was adorned with a high collar and a silk cravat. His clothing seemed to glow with an ethereal elegance, a testament to his status and success in life.

The industrialist's gaze locked onto mine. He inclined his head, acknowledging my presence.

"Miss Montgomery," he said, his voice a soft echo that seemed to reverberate through the air. "I do hope you'll excuse the intrusion, and the fact that we haven't been formally introduced. I have a message of utmost importance."

I glanced around the ballroom, taking in the bustling police officers, the frantic Quinn, and the still-irate Sylvia. Despite the commotion, it was clear that no one else was aware of the ghostly figure standing before me. I nodded at Theodore, encouraging him to continue.

His expression grew grave as he shared his message. "Miss Montgomery, there is a hidden room within this mansion," he said, his voice tinged with concern. "It has been concealed for years, known only to a select few."

Intrigued, I leaned in closer, careful not to draw the attention of those around us.

He bent down toward me and spoke urgently. "You must send your policemen to that room."

"How do we find it?" I asked.

He hesitated for a moment before continuing, "In the library upstairs, there is a wall of bookcases against the far wall. Look for the shelves just to the right of the fireplace. Behind the second shelf from the top, there is a small lever. Pull it, and my secret chamber will be revealed."

I nodded, committing the information to memory. But before I could ask any further questions, Theodore's expression shifted to one of deep concern.

"Miss Montgomery," he implored, "I must caution you. Do not step into the secret chamber yourself. Do not even peer through the doorway. The sight that awaits within is too gruesome for the fairer sex. I beg of you, bring someone with you—someone strong of heart who can withstand the horrors the room contains."

His words sent a shiver down my spine. I knew I should take his warning seriously. I promised Theodore that I would follow his advice and find someone to accompany me to the hidden room.

As I turned to seek out Jack, my mind raced with the possibilities of what might be waiting in the concealed chamber. What secrets did the enchanted Stevens Mansion hold?

As Jack and I walked up the staircase to the higher floors, we couldn't help but be captivated by the opulence of the place. Lavish tapestries and antique paintings adorned the walls, hinting at the rich history of the mansion and its previous occupants. Intricate moldings and elaborate woodwork were a testament to the craftsmanship of a bygone era.

Our footsteps echoed on the polished parquet floors. We passed beautifully carved wooden doors, each one leading to another magnificent room. Jack opened each door as we passed and glanced inside. One door revealed an elegant sitting room, its plush velvet chairs and ornate fireplace inviting us to linger. Other doors opened to reveal bedrooms with four-poster beds, and bathrooms with claw-foot tubs and Moroccan tilework.

Soon we reached the library, a room as impressive as the rest of the mansion. Towering bookshelves lined the walls, filled with leather-bound tomes that spoke of knowledge and wisdom. The scent of aged paper and polished wood graced the air as we entered.

I led Jack to the bookshelf Theodore had described, my heart pounding with anticipation. As we stood before the concealed entrance, I couldn't help but feel a mix of excitement and trepidation. What awaited us in the hidden room, and how would it change the course of our investigation?

With Jack by my side, I pulled the hidden lever. The bookshelf swung open, revealing the doorway to the secret chamber.

I hesitated for a moment, remembering Theodore Stevens' warning not to look inside—but my curiosity proved too strong to resist. With a quick, determined breath, I followed Jack inside.

Jack found a push-button light switch near the door, which illuminated an old-fashioned Edison light fixture.

As my eyes adjusted, I marveled at the room's contents.

Delicate cobwebs draped the corners of the room like gossamer lace, and a large, ornate mirror hung on one wall, its silver frame tarnished with age. There were no windows, which means there was no natural light, adding to the atmosphere of secrecy and seclusion.

As I looked around, I realized the room was a treasure trove of antiques and artifacts.

A massive, intricately carved wooden desk stood in the center of the room, strewn with yellowed papers, fountain pens, and inkwells.

In one corner, a drafting table was covered with sketches and designs of various hat styles. A collection of exotic feathers, silk ribbons, and intricate hatbands were meticulously arranged in a glass display case.

On another wall, a wooden rack held an assortment of walking sticks. Some were topped with intricate silver handles, others with ornate crystal orbs. Each one had probably been collected from Theodore Stevens' travels and adventures.

An impressive globe, its surface worn from years of use, was covered with pins and flags that marked far-flung corners of the world.

A glass cabinet held several medals and awards Theodore Stevens had received throughout his career. The gleaming gold and silver pieces were engraved with his name, reflecting the esteem in which he was held by his peers and the community.

I noticed a carved wooden box resting on a side table. I couldn't resist. I opened it and saw a collection of letters, still in their mailing envelopes, yellowed with age.

It took me just a moment to scan the room, and I knew immediately that the artifacts inside would be a priceless find for collectors and historians alike.

I felt a familiar chill in the air. Turning around, I saw Theodore Stevens' ghost flickering into view once more, his expression somber as he shook his head sadly.

"I told you not to come in here, Miss Montgomery," he said, his voice heavy with regret.

"Why? What did you think we would find, Mr. Stevens?"

Jack looked over at me, curious, waiting for me to fill him in.

The ghostly figure hesitated for a moment before gesturing towards a dark corner of the room, hidden from view by a tall, ornate screen. "There is more to this tragedy than meets the eye," he whispered, his voice barely audible.

As Jack and I approached the shadowy corner, we moved the screen aside to reveal a disturbing sight.

There, lying on the dusty wooden floor, was the lifeless body of Abigail Foster, the Wards' assistant and the manager of the Stevens Mansion.

She was still wearing the navy dress she'd worn to the fundraiser, but her clothes were rumpled, as if she had been in some kind of struggle. Several strands of her hair had fallen loose, framing her pale, lifeless face.

As I looked down at Abigail's body, the weight of the situation hit me. The painting wasn't the only thing taken during the night. Someone had also stolen Abigail's life.

# Chapter 9

I FELT A DEEP sense of sadness and shock. I had seen Abigail bustling around the mansion during the fundraiser, her efficient demeanor and warm smile a constant presence throughout the evening. It was heartbreaking to think that her life had been cut short.

I turned back to Theodore's ghost. "What do you know about all this, Mr. Stevens? Did you see what happened here?"

The ghost of Theodore Stevens hesitated again, as if weighing his words. "I regret that I was not present during Miss Foster's unfortunate demise. I do not know what rapscallion could have harmed her, or how anyone knew about my secret chamber. That being said, I will do my best to help ensure that justice is served."

I relayed the information to Jack. Then Theodore's ghost spoke once more.

"You must both tread carefully," he warned. "The secrets that lie within these walls are darker and more dangerous than you can imagine."

Jack turned to me with a serious expression on his face. "Marley, I need you to leave this room, but don't leave the premises—and don't say anything to anyone about finding Abigail's body. I'm serious about that. I don't want to jeopardize the investigation at this early stage."

We walked back the ballroom, where Quinn and Sylvia were still in distress. Jack summoned a young officer, her hair in a closely cropped Afro. "Sergeant Clark, take these three outside to that sitting area by the pool."

The outdoor entertainment area was just as elegant as the rest of the mansion. Lounge chairs were arrayed with plush cushions. Several tables were shaded by large umbrellas. A fountain burbled nearby, and the soothing sound of water lapped against the pool's edge.

Much to my surprise, Sergeant Clark guided the three of us to three separate areas around the pool, so we couldn't talk to each other. I sat at a shaded table. Sylvia settled in on a chaise lounge. Quinn stood behind a portable bar, where she helped herself to a gin and tonic. The policewoman instructed us not to speak to each other or use our phones. The detectives wanted to hear our individual accounts with no intermingling of information in advance.

The shock was apparent on all our faces. None of us expected to be treated as potential suspects in an art heist. Sylvia, her southern drawl now laced with incredulity, exclaimed, "What's all this about? Do y'all seriously think one of *us* took the painting?"

I wanted to tell them about Abigail's death and the surprise discovery of her body in the secret room, but I knew I couldn't. The weight of that knowledge sat heavy on my chest, but I had to trust Jack's judgment.

From my seat, I glanced over at Quinn and Sylvia, who both looked bewildered by the turn of events. I knew that they, like me, were grappling with the implications of being treated as suspects.

I also knew that the missing painting was just the tip of the iceberg in the larger mystery that was unfolding around us.

I looked across the yard and noticed a fleeting shadow in the windows of the carriage house. The structure looked like a cottage-size version of the mansion, with climbing ivy that led to a pitched roof. Three sets of double doors, each wide enough to admit a horse-drawn carriage, dominated the front. I imagined elegant landaus and hansom cabs pulling up to the entrance, their drivers handing the reins to waiting stable hands.

Now, however, the whole place seemed to exude an air of foreboding. I squinted and looked again. There was no sign of life in the little structure. I tuned in with my witchy senses, and I didn't detect any spirit activity, either. I chalked up the movement in the windows to the reflection of clouds in the Florida sky.

As I sat by the pool, feeling increasingly anxious and frustrated, Gregory and Hillary Ward approached. They cut through the yard to the area where we were waiting. They looked like they were dressed for a business meeting. Hillary wore a matching skirt and blazer, and Gregory was outfitted in a crisp suit and tie.

"Quinn," Gregory called out to the museum director. "Why does our home look like a crime scene? Is this about the painting? Did you call the police on us?"

Quinn merely glared at them. Sergeant Clark intercepted the Wards, leading them off to the side to speak privately. From where I was sitting, I could hear snippets of their conversation.

"I demand to know what's happening here." Hillary's voice was high pitched, as if her vocal cords were taut with indignation.

"We're conducting an investigation, ma'am," the officer replied. "I can't give you any more information."

Hillary looked angry. "This is ridiculous. We're the owners of the Stevens Mansion. We have a right to know what's going on."

Gregory rolled his eyes and shouted toward the museum director. "Honestly, Quinn, you knew we wanted the painting for the entire gala. Given all the funds we raised on your behalf, it seems downright ungrateful for you to demand its return already. We may need to rethink our donation."

Quinn furled her top lip. I might be mistaken, but I think she hissed a little, too.

Hillary looked over at Sylvia and clutched her husband's arm. "Ugh. That catering woman is here, too." She turned toward Sylvia and called out. "Did *you* call the police? Are you truly that ridiculous? We told you our assistant would mail that check you seem to need so, so desperately."

The officer spoke up. "That's enough," she said. "Please don't address any of the witnesses while we're waiting here."

Hillary sneered. "Witnesses? To what, that ghastly shrimp cocktail? Next, I suppose you'll be telling us that our guests all came down with food poisoning!" She turned toward Sylvia again and jabbed a crooked index finger in her direction. "If I hear you made any of our visitors ill, you'll be paying *us*."

Sylvia shook her head in disbelief.

The officer issued a stern warning. "Mrs. Ward, I must insist that you refrain from speaking to anyone but the investigator."

Hillary's mouth was twisted in an angry snarl. "There's no need to investigate a thing. If you'll simply locate our assistant, I'm sure she could get everything sorted out for you in no time."

The officer hesitated. "What's her name?"

Gregory bristled. "Abigail Foster, of course. I'm sure she's in the house. She's extremely reliable."

The officer shook her head. "If you'll have a seat in the gazebo, I'll have the detective meet you there."

A few more minutes passed. It probably seemed longer than it really was. Finally, another police officer approached the gazebo and addressed Gregory and Hillary,

"Mr. and Mrs. Ward, we're ready for you inside. Come with me." The Wards exchanged impatient looks before standing and following the officer into the mansion.

After what seemed like an eternity, the Wards emerged, their faces ashen. Gregory was shaking his head in disbelief while Hillary kept her eyes downcast. They didn't say a word as they reached the gazebo and sat back down.

I couldn't help but feel sympathy for them. Even though they were rude and abrasive, I knew they'd just been given terrible news. Their assistant was dead, and a priceless painting was missing. I was about to disregard my instructions and walk over to offer them a kind word. At that point, however, Jack came out to the pool.

"Marley, Quinn, Sylvia." The man was all business. "Your turn. Come on in."

We exchanged nervous glances as we followed him inside. I had no idea what we might expect in the next few minutes.

As we walked through the mansion, I felt my heart pounding in my chest. He led us into a dining room where several officers were waiting for us.

"Please have a seat." Jack gestured toward an expansive table. "We have a few questions for you."

I sit down, feeling small and insignificant. The questions were brief and to the point: he asked us about our whereabouts during the gala, if we had any contact with Abigail Foster during the party, and if we noticed anything suspicious during the evening.

I could tell that the other women were just as nervous as I was, and we answered the questions as truthfully as we could. Were we providing alibis for each other? I couldn't be sure, but everything Quinn and Sylvia said jibed with what I had seen.

The interrogations ended as quickly as they began. Jack thanked us for our time and said we could leave.

It was only as I got into my car that I realized Quinn and Sylvia were only aware of the missing artwork. They still didn't know about the murder.

# Chapter 10

As I drove back to the antique shop, my mind was racing with thoughts about the morning's events. I couldn't believe I had found myself in the middle of a murder investigation.

I had the top down on my Volkswagen convertible. It was a gorgeous Florida day, sunny and warm, with flowers blooming and birds singing in the trees. The beauty that surrounded me was a stark contrast to the heavy feeling in my heart. Abigail would never again enjoy the sun's warmth on her face or feel a breeze blowing through her hair.

As I walked into the shop, I saw Violet leaning against the checkout desk with her back against the antique brass cash register and her arms crossed. When she saw me, she put her hands on her hips.

"It's about time you got back! Eleanor and I have been running the shop single-handedly all morning."

"How could you be single-handed if there were two of you?"

She rolled her eyes. "It's not like I can do much to help on the physical plane—and Eleanor *is* elderly, you know."

She glided across the shop floor to join Eleanor at the art déco table, where the older woman had been leafing through a stack of vintage *McCall's* magazines. Then she looked at me impatiently, eyes wide, eager to hear what had happened at the mansion.

"So what's the word, bird? We know something big happened with all those old muckety-mucks. Did one of those Richie Riches kick the bucket or what?"

My grandmother came rushing in from her bakery across the street. She looked at me with concern. "We all felt a disturbance last night."

I put my purse on a shelf behind the checkout desk and took a seat at the table. "I'm not supposed to talk about this, but you'll hear the news soon. Abigail Foster was murdered last night."

Eleanor gasped. "Abigail Foster? That sweet young thing? She's one of our best customers."

I nodded. "Jack Edgewood and I found her in the mansion, in a secret room behind the library."

Violet's eyes opened wide. "Get out of town! An honest-to-goodness secret lair? I guess it makes sense, but how did you know it was there?"

"Because Theodore Stevens told me."

My grandmother raised her eyebrows in surprise. "You saw him? In person?"

"Well, in spirit, I guess."

She shook her head in disbelief. "His ghost hasn't been seen in Enchanted Springs for at least seventy years."

"Really? Interesting. But there's even more to the story. You know the painting that was unveiled at the gala last night? It's missing."

Violet looked at me. "Missing? Where did it go?"

"I don't know, Violet. That's why I said it's missing."

I pulled out my phone. "I need to call Sadie and let her know. She was at the party last night. Maybe she noticed something I overlooked."

After a few rings, Sadie answered.

"Hey, Marley. How are you feeling? Any sign of a champagne hangover?"

"I'm fine, all things considered. But I need to give you an update, and it's not good news."

"What is it? Did the Wards stiff your grandmother, too?"

"No. I don't think so. I don't know, actually. But I went back to the mansion this morning, and Sylvia and Quinn were both there."

"Yeah, Sylvia said she would be back for her check. Can you believe how the Wards treated that poor woman? I knew they were a little strange, but I had no idea they were such terrible people."

Sadie had a tendency to ask—and answer—multiple questions in a row, almost as if she was always lecturing to a classroom of students. "So why was Quinn there? Oh, I bet she wanted to get the painting. So what happened? Did Sylvia get paid?"

"No, and Quinn didn't get the painting, either."

"You're kidding. Honestly, those Wards are the worst. What did they say?"

"They weren't home. But Sadie, it's worse than that."

"What do you mean? Where did they go? Do you think they were trying to avoid Sylvia, or were they trying to avoid Quinn?"

"I don't know. Maybe both. When I got there, the Wards were nowhere to be found, the painting was missing, and then, when the police got there ... we found Abigail's body."

There was a brief pause on the other end of the line.

"You mean her unconscious body, right? Did she pass out or get sick or something? Maybe she was just overtired from all the party preparations. Is she okay?"

"No, Sadie. She's dead. I think she was murdered."

There was a brief silence on the other side of the line.

"Stop it. If you're trying to be funny, that's not a good joke."

"I'm serious. It's true. We called the police about the missing painting, and then Jack Edgewood and I found Abigail's body upstairs."

"I can't believe it."

"I know. Listen, are you home right now? I'll come over so I can fill you in on all the details. Maybe we can compare notes about what we both saw at the party last night."

***

Sadie lived in a Craftsman bungalow on a quiet, tree-lined street close to the Magnolia University campus. The house was painted blue with white trim, and the front yard was filled with colorful flowers and plants. A white picket fence surrounded the property, and a friendly "welcome" mat greeted me as I walked across the porch and stepped up to the front door.

Inside, Sadie's living room was cozy and comfortable, with cottage-style furniture and white bookshelves lining the walls. The dining room had a vintage Formica table and chairs, and the kitchen featured bright blue cabinets and old-fashioned appliances. Everything about the house suited Sadie to a T, reflecting her love of history and vintage style.

We had first met when she started working at Magnolia on an interim basis. She was filling in while my mother—also a history professor—was on sabbatical from the university. At the moment, both my mother and my stepfather were on an extended archeological expedition in Central America. I missed them, but I also hoped a full-time position would open for Sadie so she wouldn't have to find a new job when my parents returned.

Sadie handed me a glass of sweet tea, then sat mesmerized as I recounted the details of our gruesome find at the Stevens Mansion.

"I can't believe it," she said, shaking her head. "Who would do such a thing?"

We talked about the people we had seen at the party. Nothing stood out as being strange or mysterious—except for the baffling behavior of the Wards at the end of the night.

Then I told Sadie about the secret room where Jack and I had found Abigail's body.

"It sounds like something out of a novel," she said. "But it wasn't uncommon for old mansions to have hidden rooms and secret passages. Back when the Stevens Mansion was built, a lot of wealthy families wanted to have private hideaways where they could keep valuables safe."

Once again, Sadie had slipped into professor mode. Luckily, I'd grown up with professors for parents, so I was used to it.

"Some of those rooms were even used as secret passages," she said. "Usually, though, they were there for more mundane purposes, like private studies or libraries."

I nodded in agreement. "That's what I think this room was used for—but maybe you should take a look, as a historian."

"I would love to. It sounds like a treasure trove."

"I'll ask Jack if he can let us back in."

# Chapter 11

I STOPPED IN TO see Jack later that day.

The police station was a small, one-story building near the center of town. Its brick exterior gave it a sturdy, no-nonsense appearance. An American flag flew from a tall flagpole, with a Florida flag on one side and a county flag on the other. I walked through the front entrance, a plain glass door with the words "Police Department" etched in black letters.

Inside, the lobby was simple and functional, with a counter separating the public reception area from the officers' workspace in the back. The walls were lined with posters of wanted criminals and missing persons. The air was heavy with the smell of cleaning products, giving the impression of a well-maintained facility. Despite its small size, the station was well equipped with computers, radios, and security cameras.

The officer at the front desk buzzed me through a security door, and I found Jack in his office. He sat behind an oversized metal desk, a stack of files and paperwork spread in front of him. The blinds on the window behind him were closed, and his workspace was illuminated by a single lamp on the desk.

"What brings you in, Marley?"

I plopped myself down in a visitor's chair, even though he hadn't invited me to take a seat.

"I wanted to ask you about the secret room in the Stevens Mansion. My friend Sadie Arragon is one of the history professors at Magnolia University, and she's offered to assess it from a historical perspective. Do you think we could go over and see it?"

"Technically, no. The entire house is off limits for at least three days until we finish our investigation."

I frowned. "Off limits? But what about the Wards? Where are they supposed to stay? Did they get a hotel room or something?"

"Funny you should ask." He leaned back in his chair. "They actually have a condo on the beach, over near Disappearing Island."

That was odd. "Really? Like a vacation home?"

"No, like their main home. That condo is their primary residence. They don't live in the mansion."

"Of course they do. That's their big schtick. They go on and on about how they invested millions in refurbishing the Stevens Mansion and now they share their home and their wealth with the community out of the goodness of their hearts, blah, blah, blah."

He chuckled. "The truth is they're afraid to stay overnight in the mansion."

"Why?"

"Because it's haunted."

We both looked at each other for a moment, and then I laughed out loud. "They really *don't* live here, do they?"

I hadn't known the full extent of the magic in Enchanted Springs until I moved back after a few years away. When I had my Saturn Return, however, I came into my full powers. Ever since then, I could hardly make it through the grocery store without seeing at least one ghostly apparition or paranormal creature.

He shook his head sadly. "It would be funny if it weren't so sad. Right now, though, we've got a murder and an art theft to solve."

"You're right. Do you know yet how Abigail was killed?" I paused as a horrible thought struck me. "It wasn't a paranormal crime, was it?"

"No, she was shot. Not that she couldn't have been shot by a paranormal creature, but that seems unlikely."

I drummed my fingers on the arm of the chair. "That's odd, isn't it? I mean, I don't remember seeing any blood."

"There was a little, but the bullet stopped her heart instantly, so ..."

I held up my hand to stop him. Abigail and I weren't close friends, but I knew her fairly well as a customer, and I liked her. I didn't care to hear any graphic details about her passing.

I leaned forward. "Do you think Sylvia did it? Or Quinn? I noticed you didn't tell either of them about the shooting."

"We told them after you left. I'd appreciate it if you didn't discuss the details of the case with either of them."

"Okay. But you don't really think they did it, do you?"

He looked at me, expressionless.

Suddenly I remembered Julian Wainwright, and the gun he was carrying in the shop. Did he have his Colt at the gala? I couldn't remember.

"Have you spoken with Julian Wainwright?"

"Who?"

"He's a big collector of Theodore Stevens memorabilia. He flew in from Texas just to see the portrait's unveiling. He came into the antique shop yesterday to see if we had anything ... and I noticed he had a gun under his jacket."

"Why didn't you mention him before?"

"Because until this very minute I didn't know that Abigail had been shot."

Jack glowered at me, and I felt defensive. "How am I supposed to know who all the suspects are? I assumed you were making a list of everyone who was in the mansion."

"I am." He turned to his computer.

I waited for him to acknowledge me again. After a moment passed, I cleared my throat.

"So, about that secret room. When do you think we can go in with Sadie?"

I must have offended him, because he didn't warm to the idea at all. "Yeah, I'm kind of busy at the moment. I'll let you know."

He looked up from his computer and nodded his head toward the door.

"Unless you have any more suspects to tell me about, you can leave now."

# Chapter 12

As I drove away from the police station, my mind was reeling. Abigail had been shot, Julian Wainwright had been added to the list of suspects, and the Wards didn't actually live at the mansion.

In my book, that fact alone made the Wards the primary suspects. If they'd been deceptive about their home, what else had they been lying about?

I needed to clear my head and get something to eat. Gram made the best sandwiches in town, so I ducked into the Enchanted Oven for lunch.

As I stepped into the cozy bakery, I was greeted by the sweet scent of fresh baked bread. My grandmother looked up from the worktable in the back, a warm smile on her face.

"Marley, darling!" she exclaimed, giving me a hug. "How are you holding up?"

"I'm fine, Gram. Hungry, but fine."

"Sit down, sit down. I'll get you something to eat. Today's blue-plate special is chicken salad on a croissant. How does that sound?"

"It sounds perfect."

I sat at a small table in the corner and took a moment to look around the bakery. It had always been a cozy, homey space. The walls were painted a warm yellow, and a few small shelves were lined with jars of homemade jams and preserves. The scent of vanilla and cinnamon wafted from the front counter, where trays of cookies, cupcakes, and other treats were on display.

A chalkboard menu hanging over the counter listed the day's specials, including a variety of muffins, scones, and croissants. In the corner, a baker's rack held fresh loaves of bread, and I could hear the hum of the industrial mixer as Gram's assistant, Kate, worked in the kitchen.

Grandma Clara brought me a plate and took a seat across from me. The homemade croissant was buttery and flaky, the perfect carrier for her homemade chicken salad. It was a savory blend of juicy, tender chicken pieces, creamy mayonnaise, and chopped celery, along with herbs like thyme and parsley. The sandwich came with a side of sweet potato fries and a small dish of coleslaw.

I tasted the coleslaw. "This isn't your usual recipe."

She beamed. "You noticed! Yes, it's *kale* slaw, not coleslaw. Kate is really upping our game with some new recipes."

I took another bite. It was tangy and slightly sweet, with crunchy apple slices and chopped greens. I finished it before I even took a bite of the croissant.

As I ate lunch, I updated Gram on the latest developments. She listened carefully, nodding her head at all the right moments. When I finished, she leaned forward and took my hand in hers.

"Marley, my dear," she says, "you need to be careful. I know you want to help, but before you and Sadie go rushing back into that mansion, promise me you won't go inside without Jack."

"Well, of course not. Someone was murdered there, Gram."

"I know. Until they find out who killed poor Abigail, no one is safe."

She leaned in close and whispered so that only I could hear. "There are secrets in this town, Marley. Dark secrets. And some people will stop at nothing to keep them hidden."

I shivered. I wasn't used to hearing my grandmother talk as if she was a character in a mystery movie. But just as quickly, she sat up straight again, her bright smile beaming as if everything was right in the world.

"Now, what would you like for dessert?"

I asked for a single cookie, but somehow she convinced me to take two dozen assorted bars, cupcakes, and tarts with me when I left.

As I crossed the street to the antique shop, I heard the faint strains of old-time music wafting through the air. I entered to find Violet and Eleanor dancing to an old ragtime record on a wind-up gramophone.

Eleanor moved gracefully, her silver hair shining in the light as she twirled with a dexterity that defied her age. Violet's dance, meanwhile, was wild and carefree. She kicked her legs high in the air, her knees bending and straightening with each beat of the music. She waved her arms, sometimes reaching high above her head and other times extending out to her sides. Her fingers snapped in time with the rhythm, and her head bobbed and weaved as she moved around the room. Every now and then, she would let out a playful laugh.

When she saw me, she shouted a welcome. "C'mon, Marley, dance with us!"

I smiled. "You know we pay money for a streaming service, right? You don't have to listen to those scratchy old seventy-eights."

Violet rolled her eyes. "That robot music doesn't have any heart and soul, chickadee. This is music as music was meant to be heard."

I set my purse down and looked around the shop. "I wish I could, but I've already been gone most of the day. I'm sure there's a lot to catch up on."

Eleanor sat in a vintage bentwood rocker to catch her breath. "Eh. Not so much. We've had a few customers today, but nothing we couldn't handle."

"Any sales?"

She picked up her crocheting and nodded. "Mrs. Peabody bought a little angel figurine, and a cute college girl bought a fringed purse. That's about it."

Violet flopped down on a velvet settee. She looked calm, cool, and collected—but then again, she didn't have a heartbeat, so she could dance with wild abandon without getting tired.

The shop was neat and orderly. Sunlight streamed through the large display windows, casting a warm glow on the shining hardwood floors.

I did a double take. The shop was more than a hundred years old, yet the floors gleamed like new. "Did the two of you wash the floors? They look like they've been stripped and refinished."

Eleanor nodded, not looking up from her handiwork. "They have been refinished," she replied. "I called in a few house fairies who owed us a favor. They did the job overnight."

"All three levels of the shop in one night?"

"They're fairies, darling. If anything, I think they should have done the work in less time, but it's not my place to make demands of elemental creatures."

Twila had moved to Violet's side. The timeless flapper dangled a piece of Eleanor's yarn from her fingertips, tempting the spectral kitten. Twila's eyes followed its movement, then pounced.

Violet laughed and moved the yarn out of the kitten's reach, the lowered it again. The kitten pawed at the yarn, and Violet continued to dangle it teasingly. Both spirits were having a blast with their simple game.

Eleanor pulled up a second ball of yarn to change colors in her project. "How was Sadie when you saw her yesterday?"

"She wants to get into that secret room so bad she can taste it. She thinks it could be a treasure trove of history, and she wants to be the first to catalog it. Jack says we can't go in just yet, but I'm hoping he'll let us go inside at least once before the Wards get there."

"What do you mean? They live there."

I shook my head. "No. Get this: the Wards don't actually live in the mansion—because they're afraid it's *haunted*."

Violet broke out in peals of laughter. "Apparently, they don't know half of what goes on here in Enchanted Springs."

# Chapter 13

I CIRCLED MY THEODORE Stevens display, surveying it from several angles. It looked good, but I thought it could be better—especially if I could round up a few more visuals.

I sighed and mumbled to myself, "I wish we had some photos of the Stevens Mansion back when it was new."

Eleanor responded, still rocking, still crocheting. "The newsstand has plenty."

I stopped and furrowed my eyebrows. "What newsstand? Do you mean the rack at the gas station? I don't remember seeing photos for sale there."

"No, dear, the newsstand that used to stand on the corner. It was there from the 1880s through the 1950s. If you go through the storage room, you can dash back to the past and be back here in five minutes."

The suggestion was a good one, but I still wanted to think about it. When Eleanor saw me pause, she shrugged and tilted her head. "It's your call, of course."

I hesitated, because traveling through time always came at a cost. Sometimes it was an insignificant expense. A moment here or there rarely made much difference in the long run. Longer voyages, however, meant a longer readjustment period upon returning. The sensation was like waking up from a long, hard nap in the middle of the day—and over time, that recovery process could really mess with your head.

There were other factors to consider, too. The Council of Guardians who monitored our shop paid close attention to the artifacts we collected. We needed express permission to take anything that would be missed in its own time, like the first draft of *Harry Potter* or Steve Wozniak's original Apple computer. Not just verbal permission, either. Big-ticket items required written permission, in triplicate, on official paperwork that had to be signed, dated, and notarized by every member of the Council. We didn't ask for those ventures very often.

On the other hand, darting in and out of history was much simpler when it came to smaller, mass-produced items. Those were fair game, especially if they were insignificant in their own time. A few postcards from a newsstand in 1890? Completely harmless. A random assembly-line cowboy hat, purchased from a hat factory in 1872? No problem. We just couldn't tell anyone in our time where they really came from.

Eleanor carried on with her handiwork, which was shaping up to be a little crocheted version of Twila, the ghost cat. The ethereal kitten was snoozing in a sunbeam on the floor, so I could already tell that Eleanor was crafting a perfect miniature version of the cuddly creature. Eleanor had started with the cat's heart-shaped face to its long, slender tail, and she was now working her way down to the neck and shoulders. The kitten's cream-colored body and chocolate-colored points were rendered with several blends of color.

Eleanor smiled gently at me. "The choice is yours, dear. You could always find what you're looking for on one of those auction websites, too."

I thought about the trouble of searching online auctions, placing a bid, and waiting for delivery. That process seemed like more trouble than it was worth.

I took Eleanor's advice. I stepped into the storage room and closed the door behind me. I picked a random date in history, then checked a database to make sure I wouldn't step out into the middle of a violent insurrection or a raging hurricane. Then I took a deep breath and closed my eyes. I concentrated on the year 1895, picturing myself walking the streets of our quaint little town, taking in the sights and sounds of a bygone era.

In a flash, the dizzying sensation of time travel washed over me.

Moving through time was a little like being on a merry-go-round that's spinning too fast. My body felt weightless and I had to steady myself against the wall.

When the whirling sensation slowed to a standstill, I opened my eyes. I knew I was in the same dimly lit storeroom, with wooden shelves from floor to ceiling. As I looked around, however, I realized the shelves were lined with merchandise I didn't recognize, like bolts of cloth, barrels of pickles, and bags of grain.

The room smelled different, too. Instead of the earthy scent of old wood, I smelled sawdust, spices, and coffee beans. The antiques that used to be in this room had been replaced with more functional pieces, like glass jars, tin cups, and a set of scales.

I was in the 1895 version of our shop, back when it was called the Enchanted Springs Mercantile. A simple period dress was waiting for me, hanging from a hook on the wall. I slipped it over my T-shirt and shorts.

I opened the storage room door and walked out into the showroom. There were a few customers off to the side. A farmer and his son, both wearing denim overalls, were studying hand tools. Not far away, an elderly woman in a long black dress was choosing colored thread to match a fabric sample in her hand.

As I moved toward the front of the store, I was greeted by the smiling face of Martha Snow, one of my predecessors. She had been the first proprietor at the shop, and the first to guard the time portal in the storeroom. I'd met her during my first few weeks, back when Eleanor was showing me the ropes.

Martha recognized me instantly and welcomed me with open arms. "Well, if it isn't Miss Marley Montgomery!" Her eyes crinkled at the corners when she smiled, and she wrapped me in a warm embrace.

Martha was a mature woman, probably in her early sixties, with bright blue eyes that sparkled with merriment. Her hair was pulled back into a tight bun, and a few strands had fallen loose, framing her round face. She wore a frilly apron over a simple cotton dress with a floral pattern.

As she spoke, her lips turned up at the corners, drawing my attention to the dimples in her cheeks. She leaned forward and whispered, so that only I could hear, "What brings you to our little corner of the continuum?"

Like all proprietors of the shop, Martha was well versed in time travel. She had even visited our future version of the shop. Those visits were rare, however. Venturing forward in time was far more dangerous than traveling into the past. There was no way to research a trip to the future, the way we could check historical records. Most proprietors journeyed into the unknown future only when absolutely necessary. Even then, they rarely left the safety of the store itself.

I returned her smile. "Hi, Martha. I'm here on a quick errand. I've put together a display about Theodore Stevens and his hats, and I need a few period pieces."

"Oh, Mr. Stevens isn't in town right now. Enchanted Springs is only his winter home. He spends the rest of the year in Pittsburgh."

"I figured as much. I was just hoping to get some early photos of the Stevens Mansion. Eleanor said I might find some postcards at the newsstand."

She moved toward the checkout counter. "I'm sure they have plenty. They're only a few cents each. Let me get you some currency." She punched a key on the brass cash register we still used. It chimed as the cash drawer popped open.

She handed me a few silver dimes. "Take what you need. If there's any change, return it when you pass back through."

I walked out the front door of the shop and found myself on the wooden sidewalk of Enchanted Springs' familiar Main Street. I smelled tobacco smoke and fresh hay, and I heard the clanging sound of a blacksmith's hammer.

I looked down to catch sight of Twila, the ghost cat, nuzzling my legs. I gasped in surprise, then bent over to scratch the top of her head. "Did you come along for the ride, Twila, or did you exist in this timeframe too?" Twila just meowed and brushed against my ankle, her ghostly form shimmering in the sunlight before she faded from view.

In 1895, Main Street was a bustling thoroughfare, lined with wooden storefronts with large, colorful awnings. Horses and carriages passed by on the dirt road, covered with pine needles to keep the dust down. People bustled past in their Victorian-era clothing, with women in long dresses and bonnets and men in high-collared shirts.

Most people didn't notice me. While they might have been ghosts in my time, I was now a ghost in theirs. Not a full-fledged ghost, obviously, but I'd been told that anyone who looked closely at me would see me flickering as my energy phased in and out of synchronization. Psychologically, most people couldn't handle the effect. It was easier for their subconscious minds to ignore me. In a way, I was camouflaged by time itself.

I looked back at our shop. The building's exterior looked almost the same as it did in my own time. The brickwork was new, and the doors had painted lettering that read "Enchanted Springs Mercantile."

The building next to the mercantile housed a saloon with swinging doors and a large wooden sign that advertised beer and whiskey. A blacksmith's shop stood a few doors down, and next to that was a livery stable. I saw a pharmacy across the street, and a photography studio where my grandmother would someday have her bakery. I wished for a moment that I could stop in and see all the old-fashioned cameras and backdrops, but time was of the essence. That visit would have to wait for another day.

The newsstand was in a small, cramped storefront on the corner, in a wooden building with chipped white paint. Its windows were filled with various publications, from newspapers to magazines to dime novels. The inside was faintly lit by a few gas lamps hanging from the ceiling, and the walls were lined with shelves of books. The air was thick with the smell of ink and paper.

A shopkeeper, a thin and wiry man with a sharp nose, stood behind a wooden counter covered in piles of newspapers and magazines. He wore a crisp white shirt with suspenders and a bow tie, and his thinning hair was slicked back.

A few patrons ambled around the shop, browsing. One man, in a worn tweed jacket, flipped through a copy of *Sherlock Holmes*, while a woman in a blue dress scanned the cover of a *Ladies' Home Journal*. In the back of the store, a young boy with a cap on his head was admiring a collection of die-cast metal toys.

I found the postcards on a rack and picked out a few that showed the Stevens Mansion, the courthouse, and a bird's-eye view of Main Street. On a whim, I grabbed a few extra postcards for Quinn at the museum.

As I paid for the postcards, I noticed a man in a bowler hat and a tweed coat watching me intently. He had a shaggy fringe of auburn hair and a beak-like nose. I felt a sudden jolt of recognition. He looked like Calvin Carter, the art historian who spoke at the museum's fundraising gala, but this man was clean shaven. Given that Calvin's goatee was probably his most memorable feature, I had a hard time imagining that he would have shaved it off.

This particular man's presence could have been a coincidence. After all, there are a lot of red-headed men in the world, past and present.

I turned away quickly. What if it really was Calvin? Was he a time-traveler, too? If so, what was he doing here?

I didn't wait to find out. I could feel the pull of time calling me back. I hurried back into the Mercantile, hoping he wasn't following—but I had a feeling that his mysterious appearance was no coincidence.

# Chapter 14

WHEN I STEPPED OUT of the storeroom into my own time, my friend Ivy Sheridan was chatting with Eleanor. By the way she was standing near the door, I could tell she'd just walked in.

Ivy owned the biggest real-estate agency in Enchanted Springs. She had started her career as a part-time assistant, learned quickly, and soon she had founded her own company. Her offices were headquartered in the old bank building on Main Street, with marble columns in front and a balcony on the second floor.

Ivy was smart. She was beautiful, too, with long, dark hair that fell in loose waves around her face, framing high cheekbones and full lips. Her piercing green eyes were accentuated by thick, dark lashes, and she usually wore smoky eye makeup to enhance their depth.

We had known each other since kindergarten, so she didn't mince words when she saw how I looked. "Yikes, Marley. Eleanor said you were back in the storeroom, but how long did you stay in there? You look like you've stumbled out of a crypt!"

I smiled weakly, trying to shake off the minor disorientation from my quick trip to the past. "It's been a long day, Ivy," I replied, hoping to steer the conversation away from my appearance. "Longer than you can imagine." I set the postcards on a table and rubbed the back of my neck.

"In that case," she said, "you deserve a drink. I'll help you close the shop and then we can head over to Hush."

"Hush" was short for Opal Hush, our favorite wine bar.

She turned toward Eleanor. "You're invited, too, Miss Somerville! Would you like to join us for a glass of wine?"

"Oh no, dear, but thank you." Eleanor toddled over to the checkout desk and retrieved her purse, a classic black handbag with a patent leather handle. "It's bingo night at the auxiliary, so I've got to run along."

Ivy and I turned off the lights. Just before we left the shop, she pulled a small spray bottle from her purse. "I found this cucumber elixir at the farmer's market. It's a lifesaver, seriously. Close your eyes." Before I could say anything, she spritzed some on my face.

The fine mist settled on my skin, refreshing and revitalizing like a cool breeze on a hot summer day. Ivy wasn't a witch, but with this magic potion, she was the next best thing.

"It's amazing, right?" She spritzed the spray onto her own face, closing her eyes and taking a deep breath. "It's like magic. I'll buy you some so you can keep it in your purse. No offense, Marley, but you look like you could use it."

I made a mental note to ask Gram if I should tell Ivy about my abilities. In the past, our family had hidden our talents from the world, but maybe people like Ivy were ready to hear about us now.

I reached up and ran my fingers through my hair, smoothing a few tangled curls and pushing them back behind my ears. I readjusted my headband, which had slid down onto my forehead. With that, we were ready to go.

The wine bar was seamlessly incorporated into the luxurious lobby of The Springs, a historic hotel on the edge of downtown. The walls were lined with bottles of every shade and hue. Leather armchairs, velvet couches, and small tables were arranged in intimate groupings. Crystal chandeliers cast a warm light, augmented by votive candles on every table. A gentle hum of chatter filled the air, and I heard the clinking of glasses and gentle laughter among friends.

We scanned the room as we walked in and I spotted Sylvia, the caterer, sitting with a broad-shouldered man in a suit and tie. They were talking quietly.

I turned to Ivy. "There's Sylvia, the caterer from the museum gala."

"Oh, I know Sylvia! That's her husband, Manny Robinson. He leases an office in my building."

"Small world," I said.

"Small town," she agreed.

Ivy shook her head gently from side to side. "I still can't believe the Wards tried to cheat her. Don't they know her husband is a lawyer?"

"Really? I didn't know that."

Ivy grasped my elbow to lead me in their direction. "Let's go say hello."

The Robinsons looked up as we approached, and both smiled warmly.

"Ivy! What a pleasant surprise," Manny said, standing to give her a hug. "It's so nice to see you outside of work. Please, join us."

Ivy introduced me. "Manny and Sylvia, this is my friend Marley. She's the new owner of the Enchanted Antique Shop."

Sylvia turned to her husband and added, "Marley is Clara's granddaughter. We met the other night at the museum gala."

Manny shook his head sadly. "What a tragedy that evening turned out to be."

Sylvia sipped a glass of red wine. "Honestly, I thought the evening was bad enough when the Wards didn't pay me. Then they stole the museum's painting and threw murder into the mix. I can't wait until the police find whoever killed that poor woman."

Manny reached out and took Sylvia's hand, giving it a comforting squeeze. "They'll find her," he said. "And you can go on to bigger and better things."

When a waitress stopped by, Ivy and I both ordered the house cabernet.

"I still can't believe Abigail's gone," Ivy said. "She seemed like such a sweet woman."

Sylvia nodded. "She was always so kind to me. I can't imagine anyone wanting to hurt her."

Manny interjected, "Maybe it was just a random robbery gone wrong. She might have surprised someone in the act of taking the portrait."

Ivy shook her head. "The Wards are telling everyone that the whole thing was staged. They say Quinn either broke into the mansion herself to take the painting, or that she hired a burglar to do it for her."

"Are they suggesting that she killed Abigail, too?"

"They haven't come out and said it, but yeah, that's the implication."

I reached for a napkin. "That doesn't even make sense. Why would she steal her own painting?"

Sylvia looked at me directly. "Darlin', nothing those two frauds do makes any sense. Did you know they expected the museum to pay a rental fee for using the mansion that night?"

I set my glass down a little harder than I meant to. "You're kidding! They acted like they were hosting the whole fundraiser out of the goodness of their hearts."

She shook her head adamantly. "Nope. They wanted a few thousand for the space itself, with more money due for setting up, tearing down, cleaning, flowers, and insurance. They even wanted her to pay for that cheesy little microphone and speaker."

I flinched, remembering the feedback when Hillary tried to speak.

Sylvia drank the last sip of wine in her glass. "They handed her an invoice as she walked into the party. She was livid, but it was too late to back out, so she put on a brave face for everyone who came that night. You know what those Brits always say: keep calm and carry on."

I sighed. "I would be furious, but that's still not a motive for murder. Plus, how do you explain the fact that the Wards are fine? Their assistant was the one who was killed."

"If you ask me," Ivy said, sipping her water, "the Wards are the most obvious suspects. They owned the mansion. Maybe they had something to gain by getting rid of Abigail."

I shook my head. "But she did everything for them."

Ivy tilted her head. "Exactly. She knew all their secrets."

Sylvia pushed her glass to the edge of the table, signaling that she was due for a refill. "There were a lot of people at the mansion that night. Maybe the killer is someone we haven't even considered yet, someone with a grudge against the Wards, or Abigail, or maybe even the whole Stevens family."

Ivy leaned forward. "Like that rancher from Texas. He seems obsessed with Theodore Stevens."

I reached for a bowl of nuts on the table. "How did you know about him?"

"He came into the office, wondering if he could buy the mansion. We told him it wasn't for sale, but he said he's prepared to make an unsolicited offer anyway."

I raised my eyebrows. "In hindsight, that's more than a little suspicious, isn't it?"

Ivy nodded. "It almost sounds like a motive for a break-in and murder. But there's more. I looked into the county records for the Stevens Mansion, and it turns out the Wards didn't buy the property like normal people would. For some reason, Theodore Stevens' great-granddaughter just signed it over to them."

Sylvia's eyes opened wide. "How is that possible? Are you telling me they didn't pay any money for that million-dollar estate?"

Her husband reached over and took her hand. "Miranda Stevens was old and sick. There could be a legitimate reason for the transfer—but knowing the Wards, it's unlikely. It's also possible that the Wards exploited a vulnerable old woman."

Ivy nodded. "If you ask me, the whole thing stinks to high heaven."

Sylvia seemed distant, though, as if something else was on her mind.

# Chapter 15

T HE NEXT MORNING, I added my new postcards to the Theodore Stevens display. Luckily, they'd survived the trip through time without fading or yellowing.

Artifacts didn't always pass through the portal in pristine, like-new condition. I was still new to time travel, so I didn't understand the mechanics. Some items, like the *Boss of the Prairie* hat, came through unscathed. Others degraded. I'd recently gone back in time to pick up a toy yo-yo for a neighbor's eightieth birthday, and the string had rotted out completely in transit. Luckily, that part was replaceable.

I noticed a flash of light as Violet materialized in a shower of rainbow-colored sparkles. Her form coalesced gradually until she stood beside me, dressed in striped nautical top and high-waisted trousers.

She leaned in to look at one postcard, a wide view of the Stevens estate that depicted both the mansion and the carriage house in the side yard. Her nose wrinkled in disgust, as if she'd caught a whiff of something bad.

"Ugh," she said, pointing at the carriage house. "I knew the guy who lived there."

"Who? Theodore Stevens?"

"No, his driver, Charlie Frankfort."

I turned to her, encouraging her to go on. "When was this?"

She tucked a strand of hair behind her ear. "During Prohibition."

"Back when they outlawed alcohol?"

She rolled her eyes like a teenager. "Yep. What a racket. No one really stopped drinking, you know. We just stopped drinking in public."

I loved listening to Violet's stories about her party days in the 1920s. I gave her my full attention.

"Well, that booze had to come from somewhere, 'cause you couldn't exactly run out and buy a bottle of wine at the grocery store. Long story short, Vic and I did a little rum running on the side."

Vic was her husband, Victor Serrano. "Wasn't that dangerous?"

She looked down sadly. "No, not at first. I mean, we were young and dumb, but we were also just small time, bit players. And even though it wasn't legal, it was *lucrative*." She brushed her thumb against her fingertips to suggest big money in her hand.

Violet paused, her expression clouded with regret. "One day, Charlie Frankfort offered to help us expand our business. Vic wasn't sure we should trust him, but I convinced him to take the deal. Before long, we were hauling hooch across the state at least once a week."

She turned toward me. "In hindsight, that made us easy to track. When the authorities got wise, that big guy was nowhere to be found, and *we* paid the price. Vic even went to prison for a while."

I was stunned. "I had no idea."

Violet sighed. "It's all right. It was a long time ago."

She sighed. "But Charlie, that driver who organized every-thing? He got away with it all, scot-free. He still hangs out over at the Stevens Mansion, living it up like he owns the joint."

The thought of a spirit "living it up" in the afterlife seemed odd, but I think I knew what she meant.

She leaned toward me. "That ghost is bad news, Marley. That's why I haven't visited that place in years."

With that, Violet faded away. She had a tendency to disap-pear when we finished talking. Sometimes I wished she had the grace to say goodbye, but at that moment, I understood why she wouldn't have the energy.

# Chapter 16

Eleanor came in a few minutes later, breathless from her morning walk and disappointed that I hadn't made coffee yet. I started to apologize, but Eleanor stopped me, smiling.

"This is perfect! Now we can duck out for breakfast before the shop opens."

I didn't even realize I was hungry, but at the suggestion, my stomach growled in agreement. "Should we go over to Gram's?"

Eleanor peered through the window to the bakery across the street. "Oh, my, Clara looks awfully busy this morning. There could be a long wait."

"Well, we could drive up to the pancake house."

Eleanor's eyes sparkled with a mischievous glint. "We could ... but you'll never find a better breakfast anywhere than Ricky's Diner."

"I'm not sure where that is."

"Why, it's right where it's always been, back in 1956. You'll love it!"

She took my arm and propelled me toward the storeroom. After she closed the door, she assessed our clothing. Eleanor was wearing a flowered dress with short sleeves and buttons down the front. I happened to be wearing capris pants with a boat-neck sweater. "We both look rather timeless today," she noted. "We won't raise any eyebrows."

After the swirl of time travel, we found ourselves in the midcentury version of the Enchanted Antique Shop. It was still morning in 1956, which meant the shop wasn't open for business in this timeframe, either. Eleanor took some cash from the register and left an IOU in its place.

As we left the shop, a vibrant red and white Chevrolet cruised gracefully past, its sleek lines and chrome accents gleaming in the sunlight. Just a few cars behind, a turquoise Thunderbird convertable caught my attention. Its top was down, inviting the wind to playfully tousle the hair of its occupants. As it passed, I heard a few notes of a Johnny Cash song playing on the car radio, with the driver singing along about walking the line.

Ricky's Diner was a block north and a block east of the shop, in a sleek diner car with a classic chrome facade. Stepping inside was like stepping into a time capsule.

The centerpiece of the diner was a long counter lined with shiny chrome stools that spun effortlessly on their bases. Behind the counter, a serious-looking cook worked the grill, frying bacon, eggs, and sausage. My mouth watered at the irresistible aroma.

While some diners sat at the counter, others were tucked into booths with shiny vinyl seats and Formica tabletops. Each table had a jukebox selector, allowing customers to choose their favorite tunes from a selection of hits.

It definitely had a retro vibe, but since we were literally in the 1950s, I didn't know if that qualified as retro or not. The past is the past, I suppose, except when it's the present.

Two waitresses with beehive hairdos and pink aprons glided gracefully between the booths and counter, balancing trays of food and pots of coffee. The lively buzz of conversation filled the air, accompanied by the clinking of cutlery and the occasional burst of laughter.

An old Elvis song played from a jukebox—but then again, this was 1956, so technically it was a new Elvis song.

Eleanor nodded pleasantly at a few of the other customers as we took a seat in a corner booth. I couldn't tell if she knew them, or if she was simply being her usual friendly self.

Suddenly, I realized I recognized one of those other customers. While she was decades younger than I remembered her, her face was unmistakable: Mrs. Miller, the elderly librarian from my childhood, was enjoying a bowl of oatmeal at the counter. At this point in time, she wasn't an old lady with reading glasses hanging from a chain around her neck. She was a stunning young woman in an angora sweater set. She had tousled her jet-black hair into a playful flip, and she wore kitten-heeled shoes on her feet. She was reading, of course, with a book in one hand and a spoon in the other. She glanced up and out of habit, I smiled and waved. She nodded back, with only a hint of puzzlement on her face. Too late, I realized I wouldn't meet her in my own life for another forty years.

Eleanor and I settled into the booth, and I gazed out the window at people walking by. Men sported tailored suits, complete with fedora hats and polished oxfords. Women wore dresses with cinched waists, full skirts, white gloves, and pillbox hats. I felt underdressed by comparison.

A waitress handed us typewritten menus protected by clear plastic sleeves. I studied the options, then looked at Eleanor, who had already put her menu down on the damp, freshly wiped tabletop. "I'll probably just get toast and coffee," I said. "But these prices are incredible. Bacon and eggs for seventy-five cents? Pancakes for thirty cents?"

"You'll probably want to order a full breakfast, dear. Most of what we eat in the past burns off during the return trip."

I raised my eyebrows in surprise.

"I know," she said. "Calories hardly count on the continuum. It's a dieter's dream."

The waitress took our order and filled our coffee cups. I added cream to my coffee, then stirred it with my spoon. I whispered, hoping no one could hear us.

"So it's totally okay to dip into the past for meals?" I asked.

Eleanor sipped her coffee. "Meals, movies, concerts ... It's one perk of being a proprietor. As long as we don't do anything to interfere with the timeline, it's allowed."

"But what if we're sitting at a table someone else was destined to use? Wouldn't that trigger some sort of butterfly effect?"

"Look around, Marley. There are at least three empty tables in this diner. History isn't so fragile that we can't squeeze in for a bite to eat. Now, if we were to intentionally disrupt the timeline, we might have a problem."

I leaned forward with my elbows on the table. "There's something I've been dying to know. Why couldn't we travel back in time to the night of Abigail's murder, just so we could see who killed her? I understand we couldn't stop the murder. I mean, it seems unfair, but it is history. But why can't we at least go find out who killed her, so the murderer can be brought to justice?"

Eleanor spooned sugar into her cup, then stirred. "There are times when we can serve as an eyewitness to history. There are even times when we *should* be on hand to ensure that the truth can be told." She took a bite of toast. "But in our time, now that poor Abigail has been killed, the sequence of events is already in progress. We need to let destiny run its course without interference."

"I find it hard to believe that it was Abigail's destiny to be murdered. It seems so unfair."

"I understand, dear. It's not always easy to watch history unfold, especially when you know where it's going."

We were silent for a few minutes as our food arrived. After I plowed my way through half a stack of fluffy buttermilk pancakes with butter and syrup, I came up for air.

"Just out of curiosity, what would happen if I tried to change history? Would I be killed?"

Eleanor cut her bacon with a knife and ate a bite with her fork. I wondered if I could ever be so classy.

"Killed?" She looked at me with her eyes wide in shock. "Oh, heavens, no, of course not. Nothing so crass."

"Would I be hurt?"

She shook her head. "Not intentionally. The Council of Guardians isn't a vindictive organization."

"Would I be punished?"

She took another sip of her coffee and chuckled softly. "Only if you deliberately interfered with the timeline. Even that would be highly unlikely, though."

"How so?"

"There are cosmic safeguards in place to ensure that proprietors can't simply dabble about. If you traveled back to save Abigail—theoretically speaking, of course—you'd run into any number of obstacles. You probably couldn't interfere no matter how hard you tried."

"What do you mean?"

"Well, you'd be stopped in your tracks. You could find yourself trapped in an infinite time loop. You'd experience the same course of events, day after day, week after week, until you managed to return to your own time."

"To be honest, that sounds a little vindictive."

"Unless it lands you a movie deal. That odd little Ghostbusters man made millions when he had his whole groundhog experience."

"Wait, what?"

"Oh, that's not important right now. You wanted to know what might happen to you, right?"

I swiped up the last bit of syrup on my plate with an oversized bite of pancake. "Mmmph," I mumbled, my mouth too full to talk.

"You could be redirected. I won't go into the details, but there was a time when I thought I could nip an old philosophy book from the Biltmore Estate. Instead of landing in North Carolina, I was dispatched to North Dakota. Good lord. I've never been so cold in all my life."

She laughed. "Then again, you might simply rebound and find yourself bounced right back to your own time without seeing a thing."

She took a last swallow of her coffee, draining the cup. Then she used a paper napkin to dab the corners of her mouth.

"Personally, the worst thing I've experienced is fractalization, when I found myself in the center of multiple timelines at once. It was like being in a funhouse, surrounded by mirrors." She sighed. "It was the opposite of fun."

The waitress came by with the check. Eleanor counted out the exact change and left a dime for a tip.

As we stood, she took a deep breath and looked at me serious-ly. "Honestly, there's no end to what *could* happen, which is why it's best to play by the rules."

# Chapter 17

O N  T H E  W A L K  B A C K  to the shop, I asked if I could try revisiting the fundraising gala.

"I think I'm ready to step up my game. So far, all of my training trips have been light, bright, and easy. Not that I'm complaining about breakfast, of course. Ricky's Diner was fantastic."

As if to reinforce my point, I accidentally burped a little. I hoped Eleanor hadn't noticed my syrup-scented belch, so I kept talking as if nothing had happened. "I'd really like to go back to that gala at the Stevens mansion."

"Oh, Marley, that could be dangerous. You'd be mingling with a murderer."

I nodded. "Technically, I suppose that's true, but I was never the target. I haven't been back in Enchanted Springs long enough to make any mortal enemies."

She looked at me with a serious look in her eye. "If you went back to that party, you'd be on the lookout for trouble. That alone might be enough to get you on the killer's radar."

"What if I took Sadie along? They always say there's safety in numbers. She was also there the first time, so that wouldn't disrupt the timeline at all."

"Oh, no. The Council of Guardians has been clear. Only the shop's proprietors are allowed to use the portal."

"Eleanor, you and Gram have gone on missions together. It seems unfair that I don't have a travel partner."

Eleanor looked at me, her blue eyes searching and innocent. "You have me."

I realized too late that I'd hurt her feelings. "Yes, and you're a terrific mentor. But I took this job so you could retire. How long has it been since you've had a vacation?"

She looked up and to the left as if she was trying to remember. "Vacations? Well, I've had plenty of adventures along the time-line."

"But no actual vacations."

"Now that you mention it, I have had my eye on a cruise to Aruba. And your grandmother has been talking about a bus tour of England."

"See, you deserve the freedom to take off and live your life without feeling responsible for me or the portal."

She nodded, considering.

I decided to argue my case just a little more. "You'll never find a more talented spellcaster than Sadie, or a more experienced historian. If the time ever comes when you and Gram want to take trip around the world, you could trust the two of us to safeguard the portal. Not that we wouldn't welcome your help, but just imagine how freeing that would be."

"You don't have to sell me on Sadie's gifts. I've known for many years that she is one of the most capable witches of your generation. It's your grandmother that might need some convincing. Let me talk with her."

The minute we were back in our own time, Eleanor toddled across the street to the bakery, and I texted Sadie to come to the antique shop. As we waited, I outlined my plan to include her in a trip back to the fundraising gala.

Sadie was too excited to sit still. She paced between the checkout desk and the front windows, trying to see what Clara and Eleanor were discussing. "If only I could read lips," she said. She ran her fingers through her hair and sighed. "They look so serious. They're probably trying to figure out how to say 'no' without hurting my feelings."

Minutes passed like an eternity before Clara and Eleanor emerged from the bakery, their faces filled with determination. They walked back to the Enchanted Antique Shop, and as they entered, I could sense a newfound resolve within them.

Clara's voice held a hint of authority as she spoke, "Oh, Sadie, you're here. Good. Eleanor and I wanted to talk to the two of you, together."

Sadie and I both held our breath. We knew I had asked for a lot, and we were prepared for a kind but firm rejection.

My grandmother looked at both of us, first one, then the other, studying our faces seriously for what seemed like an eternity.

Finally, Eleanor broke the tension. She leaned forward with a broad grin and clasped Sadie's hands in hers.

"Sadie, my darling. How would you like to join us at the antique shop as an associate proprietor?"

# Chapter 18

SADIE WAS IN SEVENTH heaven. "Seriously? Yes! When Marley told me what you were discussing, I almost lost my mind. This is a dream come true!"

Sadie beamed. Sadie was practically vibrating with nervous energy. "This is so exciting," she whispered. "I've never traveled back in time before. I've heard temporal witches talk about it, but I always thought it was absolutely forbidden for other magical practitioners."

"It's an unconventional move, but it makes sense. Eleanor and I have operated as a team for many years. At the moment, Marley is the only temporal witch of her generation—but your spellcasting abilities complement her abilities nicely. We've also been impressed by your passion for history."

At that point, I noticed Clara had brought a cake with her. "Even though it's spur of the moment, I thought we should be prepared to celebrate."

Oddly enough, I was hungry again. Eleanor had been right. It felt like my entire breakfast had burned off already, probably over the sixty-some years we traveled that morning.

As Eleanor sliced and served the triple-layer red velvet dessert, Clara outlined the rules of time travel.

"First, you must maintain history's integrity. Don't try to change the course of events. Don't interfere with the sequence of events. No messing with the timeline."

"I would never!" Sadie exclaimed.

"Second, you may not remove artifacts that would be missed in their own time."

"I might need direction on that one. Collecting antiques is one of my passions."

Eleanor nodded. "We can help you with that."

"Third, don't interfere with the flow of time by revealing information about the future."

"Understood."

"For your first few trips together, your time will be limited, and you'll be closely monitored."

I leaned forward. "So we can go back to the Stevens Mansion?"

"You'll have thirty minutes, total, to look around. This isn't a chance for you to investigate or ask questions. It's a training exercise, so you can get a feel for visiting consequential moments in history."

Clara furrowed her brow intently. "And just to make sure nothing goes awry, you'll be traveling with a chaperone."

"You mean, with you? Or are you talking about Eleanor?"

"No, that would defeat the purpose of letting you test the waters without us. You'll be accompanied by one of our other trusted partners here at the shop."

With that, a soft whisper of air blew into the room. I turned around to see a small point of light growing larger, like an iridescent bubble filling with cosmic energy. It was illuminated from within, and as it grew, it pulsed with all the colors of the rainbow. I watched, mesmerized, as it cast beams of light throughout the shop. Red, orange, green, yellow, and blue ... and then it popped, and Violet stood in front of us.

"Hello, besties!" She greeted us with a mischievous grin, her voice tinged with excitement. "I hear we're going on an adventure."

I looked at my grandmother. "Seriously? Violet is our chaperone?"

She put her hands on her hips. "Would it be easier to think of me as your caretaker?" Then she laughed. "Maybe you should refer to me as your guardian and protector. It's all the same to me. Just know that as we go back in time, I'll have your back."

"It is for the best," Gram added. "Violet can keep an eye out for hidden dangers that the two of you might not see."

"Fair enough." I looked at Sadie. "Are you ready? Do you want to take a practice trip to some other point in the past?"

"Marley, I was born ready. Let's dive right in."

I looked at Sadie's outfit, then my own. We were both in our everyday clothes. I was still in my boatneck sweater and capris, and Sadie wore a white blouse with black trousers.

I gestured at our outfits. "If we go like this, we'll stand out like a sore thumb. Everyone dressed up for the unveiling."

"No problem," Sadie said. "I can cast a quick glamour over us. If you don't mind my saying so, we looked pretty great that night."

She raised her right hand and twirled her index finger to send energy swirling gently around us.

*As we travel back in time,*
*Magically, our forms align.*
*We'll look just like we did that night,*

*Clothed in magic and in light.*

As she cast her spell, I could feel a cool breeze stirring through the space. In less than sixty seconds, our magical makeovers were complete. Our hair was styled, our casual clothes became cocktail dresses, and our makeup was expertly applied. We looked just as elegant as we did the night of the gala.

I looked at Sadie. "Why can't you do this every time we go out?"

She laughed. "Because it's a temporary illusion. I'm pretty good at glamourizing, but I can't guarantee this look will last more than an hour or two."

I reached down to smooth my skirt, but when I felt my slacks instead, I realized that my dress was merely an optical illusion.

"I do cast a pretty good glamour spell, even if I say so myself."

"Are you ready?"

She took a deep breath and nodded.

"You might want to hold onto a wall or the shelves or something for support. This part can feel a little intense, especially when it's your first time."

# Chapter 19

I CLOSED MY EYES and pictured us standing outside the Stevens Mansion on the night of Abigail's murder.

When we both opened our eyes, we were once again on the lawn, surrounded by twinkling fairy lights. We could hear music and lively chatter coming through the open windows of the mansion.

Sadie looked a little green. "You weren't kidding!" she exclaimed. "Hold on while I catch my breath. I do *not* want to throw up in the flowerbeds."

Violet materialized next to us, in a red sequined dress that showcased her slim build and long legs. It was loose and straight-cut, with a hem that fell just below her knees. Her arms were loaded with bangle bracelets. A feathered headband highlighted her bobbed hair, and a long, pearl necklace swayed with every move she made.

She watched impatiently as we acclimated. "You know the clock is ticking, right? Shake a leg already. Just take a few deep breaths, Sadie, and you'll be good to go."

When we knocked on the door, the butler seemed surprised to see us. Well, surprised to see Sadie and me. I was pretty sure Violet was invisible, even in her eye-catching flapper attire.

"Welcome back, ladies. You must have stepped out when I wasn't looking." He bowed and with a sweeping gesture invited us into the foyer.

Abigail seemed perplexed, too. She was wearing the navy dress I remembered, and I noticed how her vintage brooch reflected the light of the chandelier. She shook her head slightly, as if she was questioning her own two eyes. "I could have sworn the two of you just came in."

It was so bittersweet to see her standing there, alive and well, knowing what fate awaited her later that night. If only I could give her some sort of warning. The minute that thought flashed through my mind, a searing pain tore through my head, as if I'd been jolted by a bolt of lightning. I gasped.

Sadie covered for me. "We did just come in. Once we got into the ballroom, I realized I'd forgotten my earrings in the car, so we ducked out the side door to get them."

"Ah," Abigail smiled. "They're lovely. Well, it's nice to meet you, again. Maybe we can all get together some time to talk about antiques, and history, and the Stevens Mansion."

Sadie and I both sighed wistfully. "That would be wonderful. I really wish we could."

We walked back toward the ballroom. "What happened to you back there?"

"It was the strangest thing. I wondered, just for a moment, if I could caution Abigail to be careful tonight. Just the thought of it, however—" Suddenly, the pain struck again.

Sadie yelped, too. "Ouch! Marley, are you doing that?"

I rubbed my temples. "No, not on purpose! That must be some sort of cosmic fail-safe mechanism. So clearly, we're not allowed to interfere with the timeline in any way. Just thinking about it makes my head hurt."

She ran her fingers through her hair. "That's worse than an ice-cream headache. What do you suppose would happen if we managed to say anything at all?"

"We'd probably stroke out." I took a deep breath. "Okay. Let's try to move forward and see if we can keep our impulsive thoughts under control and revisit this party without giving ourselves a brain bleed."

We reached the ballroom, but when we tried to move through the doorway, the room seemed to push us back. It felt like an invisible force field had sealed the entry.

Sadie and I exchanged bewildered glances. "Why can't we go in?" Sadie whispered.

"I'm not sure. Let's try another way."

We meandered through the mansion, attempting different routes. Whenever we encountered other party goers, they greeted us with puzzled expressions.

One of Sadie's colleagues stopped in his tracks and asked, "Didn't I just see you by the fireplace?" Someone else looked at me curiously and said, "How did you get here so fast?" A third person did a double-take and said, "I could have sworn I passed you a second ago, standing by the portrait."

Several entry points led into the ballroom, but they were all blocked. We moved from doorway to doorway, catching glimpses of the gala from different angles. We could hear fragments of conversations and snippets of laughter. We could see plenty of familiar faces. We could even see the portrait, still veiled by its red velvet drape. We simply couldn't enter the room. Every time we tried to approach the heart of the party, we hit that invisible force field.

"I get it," Sadie said. "They say you can't be in two places at once, but in time travel, you can't have two versions of yourself in the same place at the same time."

I nodded. "That makes sense. It's so weird to think that two other versions of ourselves are in that room, but we can't see them."

"And no one else can see the two simultaneous versions of us, either."

Periodically Violet would zip away and then report back with news from the ballroom. "Marley, you're talking to that tall drink of water from Texas. And Sadie, you're at the buffet." Violet stopped to sweep her eyes up and down Sadie's figure. "Sweetie, you just ate your way through three cream puffs, two eclairs, and a full-size roast-beef sandwich."

Sadie stood a little straighter, as if she'd been praised. "Stick around. When I go back for seconds, you'll see me hit the seafood station for a few rounds of shrimp cocktail and then the cheese table for dessert."

Violet high fived her. "That's quite the magic dress you wore. I'm surprised it didn't split at the seams."

"Yeah, it's some sort of stretchy polyester blend. It's too bad I can't get into the ballroom again. I could really go for a few mini quiches and maybe some of that fruit salad."

I sighed. "Well, this has been an interesting experiment, but clearly we're at an impasse."

"Agreed. Plus I'm hungry. How do we get back?"

"The same way we came. Let's find a quiet place where I can focus."

We stepped out into the yard through a side door, then ducked behind the carriage house where no one could see us. I held Sadie's hand and closed my eyes, and once again we were in the storeroom.

# Chapter 20

I OVERSLEPT THE NEXT morning. Visiting my own recent past at the Stevens Mansion took more energy than I would have imagined.

I took a deep breath as I adjusted to the sights and sounds of the modern world around me. The sun was shining, birds were singing, and the charming streets of my small hometown were alive with the rhythm of everyday life. Everyone seemed to have a purpose for being out and about, and most looked happy and content.

I felt more grounded as I walked to work, too. The echoes of the past still whispered in my mind, but I was regrouping with the present. I stopped in at the shop to grab the antique postcards I'd picked up for Quinn, then headed off to the Enchanted Springs Museum of Art.

The building itself was a work of art. The museum was housed in a former department store that had been designed to impress. In recent years, the brickwork on the exterior had been painted cream, with contrasting bands of green and tan. The door was framed with roman columns, and the windows were topped with arched pediments.

I stepped through the double doors and savored the scent of old brick and plaster, along with floor cleaner and wood polish. I also detected the subtle, sweet aroma of pipe smoke, even though smoking had been banned indoors for years.

The original hardwood floors had been sanded and refinished to look like new. High ceilings and a grand staircase drew the eye up to exhibit space on each level.

I took a few steps into the lobby, where an elderly woman stuffed envelopes at the reception desk. I glanced at her nametag, which read *Edith Marsh, Volunteer.*

"Are you a member, dear?" I nodded, and she smiled. "Please sign in."

I followed banners and posters to the Theodore Stevens exhibit designed to showcase the new portrait. An empty wall made it clear where the painting was supposed to hang. For now, there was a small photo instead, along with a news story about the missing artwork.

I wandered around a bit, joining a few other museum visitors who were browsing a display of related memorabilia. The walls were adorned with vintage advertisements and old photos of cowboys wearing their Stevens hats in rugged western terrain.

A series of glass cases displayed an impressive collection of iconic Stevens hats and colorful hat boxes. I recognized the classic cowboy hats right away, but I was amazed by the other styles and colors, including fedoras, bowlers, and women's hats.

Moving deeper into the exhibit, I saw some of Stevens' original hat-making tools, with machines from the late 1800s used to shape the felt and trim the brims. In one corner, an interactive display allowed visitors to touch and feel different hat materials, including beaver, rabbit, and wool felt. Nearby, a video screen played interviews with modern-day hat makers discussing Theodore Stevens' legacy.

There was even a small display of Stevens family photos. One hand-colored image depicted Theodore's mother, a young woman with a cleft in her chin, beaming at her three-year-old son. Quinn had clearly put a lot of thought and effort into creating a cohesive and engaging exhibit.

She came out of her office just as I was headed in to say hello.

"Hey, Quinn. How are you holding up?"

"It's been rough," she admitted. "I can't wait until they find who took the painting." She hastily added a follow-up. "And arrest Abigail's killer, of course."

I reached into my bag and showed Quinn the postcards I'd carried over. "I found these in our storage room," I said. "We had several copies, so if you'd like them for your display, you're welcome to keep them."

She admired them briefly without taking them out of their plastic sleeves. "They're wonderful," she said. "Let's just have you fill out a donation form."

At that moment, however, we were interrupted by the sound of heavy footsteps. I watched in shock as Jack Edgewood strode toward us, his hand already reaching for the handcuffs on his belt. My heart sank as I saw him approach. I could tell by the grim expression on his face that something was very wrong.

"Quinn Delaney, I have a warrant for your arrest. You're being charged with the murder of Abigail Foster."

Quinn's face went pale with shock and disbelief. "What are you talking about?"

Jack didn't falter. "I'm sorry, Quinn, but we have evidence that links you to the crime."

I stepped forward. "Wait a minute. Do you honestly think Quinn killed Abigail? That's ludicrous. It's not like she needed to murder anyone to get that painting back. It belongs to the museum."

"Marley, stop. Quinn, you'll have to come with me."

Quinn protested vehemently. "I wouldn't hurt anyone. I couldn't hurt anyone. I only wanted to get the painting back."

He held up a hand to stop her from saying anything more. "I must advise you that you have the right to remain silent." Like a scene from a television show, I watched open-mouthed as Jack read Quinn her Miranda rights.

Her face twisted in disbelief as Jack snapped handcuffs on her wrists.

She looked me in the eye as she passed. She seemed surprisingly calm. "Quinn," she said, enunciating every word. "Please call my lawyer and ask him to meet me at the police station." She turned to Jack. "We are going to the police station, correct?"

Jack nodded, and Quinn continued. "Indeed. Please call my barrister, Charles Phillip Marsh. Let him know what's happened."

I was already reaching for my phone. The Marsh law firm was well-known in Enchanted Springs.

As Jack led Quinn away, I couldn't help but feel a pang of sadness for her. She may have seemed feisty and unflappable on the outside, but I saw the fear and uncertainty in her eyes. I followed them out of the museum, trying to process what had just happened.

Gregory and Hillary Ward were standing on the sidewalk, watching the scene unfold with satisfaction. Gregory raised his chin triumphantly as Jack escorted the museum director past them to a waiting police car. "Thanks for your quick response, officer. Now take that crazy Brit to jail. Bye-bye, Miss Tea-and-Crumpets! Serves you right!"

Hillary bobbed her head up and down as if she'd just won a wrestling match. "I told you she was guilty," she said, her voice dripping with disdain.

Quinn pretended not to hear. Jack put his hand on the top of her head so she wouldn't bump it on the car frame. "Don't worry," he said. "You'll have your chance to tell your side of the story." He closed the door gently, and I heard the automatic locks engage.

As they pulled away, I was left standing on the sidewalk, feeling stunned.

# Chapter 21

WITH NOTHING ELSE FOR me to do at the museum, I walked back to the antique shop. I called Sadie on the way to update her on the latest development.

She answered after a few rings, her voice filled with warmth and curiosity. "Hey there, Marley! What's going on?"

I took a deep breath. "Sadie, you won't believe what just happened. Jack just arrested Quinn for Abigail's murder."

There was a brief silence on the other end of the line, and I sensed Sadie's shock through the phone. "That's ... that's unbelievable. Were you there? How do you know? What happened?"

I sighed, my footsteps slowing as I continued down the sidewalk. "I was at the museum, talking to Quinn, when Jack came in and placed her under arrest. It was like something out of a mystery novel. I couldn't believe my eyes."

Sadie's voice held a mixture of concern and disbelief. "Do they have any evidence? Is there any reason to suspect Quinn?"

I shook my head, even though she couldn't see me. "I don't know, Sadie. They must have found something, but I can't imagine Quinn ever being capable of such a thing."

She paused, and I could practically hear the wheels turning in her mind.

"Well, if there's been an arrest, the Wards are probably back in the mansion again."

I nodded, even though she couldn't hear me over the phone.

"Marley, I really want to get into that secret room before anyone dislodges any of the artifacts in there."

"I agree. I mean, I know the police have combed through it all, but what if there's evidence they overlooked? They weren't looking at it from a historian's point of view."

A few minutes later, Sadie joined me at the shop.

"We need to get back into that mansion before the Wards can get their hands on those artifacts. We can't afford to let those valuable pieces of history slip away or be mishandled."

I nodded in agreement. "You're right, Sadie. But how?"

We shared a moment of silence, lost in our own thoughts.

Behind us, Hazel Turner cleared her throat.

She worked so diligently that I hadn't even noticed she was in the shop. The unassuming cleaner had been quietly going about her work, moving discreetly in the background, dusting shelves and sweeping floors.

I looked at her in shock. "Hazel! You're here! I'm sorry I didn't see you earlier. I forgot it was your day to come in."

She smiled gently. "We've all been thrown for a loop by poor Abigail's murder."

"I couldn't help but overhear your conversation," she continued, her voice tinged with curiosity. "Are you two talking about the Stevens Mansion?"

I nodded in response, then remembered other conversations I'd had with her. "That's right! You clean for the Wards, too."

"I do." Hazel used a spray bottle of blue cleanser to dampen a soft cleaning rag. "I'd always heard rumors of secret rooms in the mansion." Her voice was filled with intrigue. "In all my years of cleaning, though, I've never seen any sign of them. It's always been a mystery to me."

Hazel was a petite woman with a wiry frame and a sprightly demeanor that defied her fifty-odd years. Her gray hair was styled in a long braid down her back. Deep lines etched the corners of her eyes. Her hands were weatherworn from years of cleaning. Her nails were cut short, and the only jewelry she wore was a plain gold wedding band.

Hazel's clothing, simple and practical, reflected her no-nonsense approach to her work. She dressed in faded denim jeans, a plain white T-shirt, and a navy-blue apron with pockets.

She put the bottle back in her cleaning tote. "In fact, the police just released the crime scene at the mansion, and I'm scheduled to go over there today."

She gazed up at the ceiling, as if she was picturing herself in the mansion. "To be honest, I dread going in there. I know they assured me there's no trace of blood or anything gruesome, but still ..."

I tried to look calm as I realized the opportunity that lay before us. "Hazel, you shouldn't have to face that by yourself. Would you like us to go with you?"

Hazel's face lit up with relief. "Oh, that would be wonderful! The Wards have already told me they won't be there, so I'd have to go in all alone." She shuddered slightly. "If you two wouldn't mind, I'd appreciate your company."

# Chapter 22

AS WE STOOD AT the back door of the majestic Stevens Mansion, Hazel Turner's keys jingled in her hand, ready to unlock the secrets that lay within its walls.

Our anticipation grew as Hazel led us up the back staircase, our footsteps echoing in the narrow passageway. When we reached the third floor, the library beckoned us, emanating an air of mystery.

Hazel stood in the hallway, her gaze fixed on the paneled doors. She took a deep breath, her trembling hands clutching her cleaning supplies. I saw the anxiety etched on her face.

"I just ... I can't go in there," Hazel whispered, her voice quivering. "I've been dreading this moment, seeing the place where poor Abigail ... you know."

Sadie placed a comforting hand on Hazel's shoulder. "It's okay, Hazel. Marley and I can go in first, just to make sure there's nothing too upsetting."

I nodded in agreement, offering a reassuring smile. "Absolutely. We'll take a quick look and make sure it's all right. You don't need to worry."

Hazel's eyes filled with gratitude, a mixture of relief and apprehension. "Thank you, both of you. I appreciate your kindness."

Sadie and I entered the library, leaving Hazel in the corridor outside the double doors. As we crossed the threshold, the scent of old books enveloped us, the room steeped in a sense of history. I glanced at Sadie, and we shared a silent understanding of the importance of this moment.

As we cautiously opened the hidden door and entered the secret room, a wave of relief washed over us. The concealed chamber showed no signs of disarray or disturbance. The quiet space stood in stark contrast to the unsettling events that had unfolded within its walls. We exchanged glances of reassurance, grateful that we would all be spared from any tangible reminders of the crime.

As we walked back out into the library, Hazel looked at us expectantly. "Is it ... all right?"

I smiled warmly at her. "Yes, Hazel. It's okay. You can come in."

Her tense shoulders eased, and a flicker of gratitude shone in her eyes. "Thank you both. I don't know what I would do without your support."

Hazel's jaw dropped when she saw the secret room behind the fireplace. It truly was a stunning sight. In addition to the desk and drafting table I had seen before, this time I noticed a mahogany chair, expertly carved with intricate patterns and ornate details. I spotted a framed lithograph that showcased a bustling street scene of nineteenth-century Pittsburgh, with horse-drawn carriages, dapper gentlemen in top hats, and ladies with parasols. Along one wall, a vintage cigar humidor still held several cigars, each wrapped with a colorful paper band.

The secret room was still dusty, of course. We all noticed the footprints and track marks where Abigail's body had been found and investigators had walked around the room.

Hazel looked at the floor uncomfortably. I sensed her unease as she glanced at her cleaning supplies. "Should I mop or sweep?" she asked, her sense of duty conflicting with the delicate nature of the situation.

Sadie placed a comforting hand on Hazel's arm, offering reassurance. "At the moment, you don't need to do either. Because this is a historical site, I'd like to document the antiques and artifacts exactly as they look right now."

Hazel nodded, a grateful smile gracing her face. "I'll leave you to it, then," she said. "It'll take me about three hours to do the rest of my cleaning. If you need anything, let me know."

Sadie looked at me and described her plan. "It's like an archeological dig," she explained. "We want to document the position of everything we see here before we move any of the artifacts."

Her eyes sparkled with enthusiasm as she explained. "We'll have to be as thorough as possible, because there's no telling if or when we'll ever get a chance to come in here again. Let's try to gather as much information as possible."

At Sadie's instruction, I had grabbed my camera gear from home. She pointed to the corners of the room, then swept her arm broadly to indicate the walls adorned with faded wallpaper and intricate moldings. "First, let's start with overall photographs," she instructed. "Take wide shots of the room from different angles."

I nodded, clicking my camera into action and framing each shot. The soft click echoed through the room, freezing moments in time on my camera's digital memory.

"Next," Sadie continued, "we'll focus on the finer details. Look for any unique elements or artifacts that might offer clues about the room's purpose or the people who once inhabited it."

She pulled a measuring tape from her purse. "In studies like this, it's important to have a reference point in the photos. That way, we'll be able to show the scale of the artifacts and the architecture."

With Sadie's guidance, I positioned the measuring tape next to the items I photographed—a small figurine, an ashtray, a collection of old books on a shelf. I captured close-up shots, too, allowing the camera to reveal the intricate carvings on the desk.

I opened the desk drawers, both to take photos of their contents and because I was curious about what they might hold. I couldn't escape the feeling that I was prying, even though the owner of the desk had been dead for more than a hundred years. It felt like I was disturbing a grave.

Most of the drawers held what you'd expect to find in any desk. I noticed pencils, notepaper, and old letterhead stationery, imprinted with Theodore Stevens' name. The office supplies were more than a century old, so instead of ballpoint pens, there were fountain pens and inkwells, the ink long since evaporated.

The bottom drawer, however, wasn't a drawer at all. When I pulled the handle, it opened like a door, revealing a small safe, complete with a numbered dial. I grazed it with my fingertips and watched in amazement as the dial turned itself, as if it was being spun by an unseen hand.

With a click, the safe opened, revealing a stack of stock certificates and bond notes. I reached out to touch them, but Sadie stopped me.

"Hold on," she said, pulling two pairs of white cotton gloves from her purse. "You shouldn't touch any paperwork in here with your bare hands. We need to protect these artifacts."

"Do you just walk around with gloves in your purse?"

"I do. In my line of work, you never know when you're going to handle archival materials."

I slipped on the gloves and riffled through the stack of documents. Most featured elegant illustrations and vignettes of railroads, oil fields, and manufacturing plants.

Something rattled in the bottom of the safe, and I reached down to retrieve a velvet pouch, tied closed with a silk drawstring. I handed it to Sadie. She tugged at the drawstring to open it and gasped. The pouch was filled with antique silver dollars.

I used my phone to check the value of the coins. I had to double, then triple-check the markings on each one.

"Sadie," I whispered, my voice feeling hoarse with excitement. "I think these coins are worth millions."

"Take pictures," she said, "and we'll put everything back the way we found it."

It seemed like it took forever to snap all the photos Sadie wanted. At long last, after she reviewed the most recent series of photos I'd taken, she nodded with satisfaction. "Those are good," she said. "Let's switch to video."

My camera could shoot still photos or video, so that was no problem. "Sure. That way, we'll have an overall view of how everything fits together."

Sadie pointed to different areas of the room. "Start by recording a walkthrough of the space, capturing the layout from different angles. Show the walls, the ceiling, and the floor. Then zoom in to the furniture and the smaller artifacts."

I adjusted the settings on my camera and started recording, panning across the room to capture the intricacies of its design. Sadie provided commentary as we went along, explaining and sharing her observations.

As we continued our exploration, Sadie directed me to film specific areas of interest. Her enthusiasm was contagious. By the time we were finished, we could see the room as a time capsule, rather than the site of a recent tragedy.

Sadie checked her watch. "We're still good on time. Let's look at some of these letters."

I picked up the box, feeling the weight of it in my hands. It was crafted of dark, exotic ebony wood, and I marveled at its intricate carvings of vines and flowers. It was heavier than it looked.

I carried it out to the library, where the light was better, and we sat down at an oak table. Sadie slipped on a pair of gloves and we exchanged excited glances.

She lifted the lid, revealing a treasure trove of correspondence. Bundles of envelopes were neatly arranged and tied with delicate ribbons. Each letter seemed like a portal to history, bridging the gap between the past and the present. The scent of aged paper filled the air, along with a hint of something I couldn't quite place. Was it tobacco? Pipe smoke? Aftershave? It was very faint, and not at all unpleasant.

Sadie pulled the first letter out of the box. Its edges were yellowed with age. I noticed old-fashioned cursive script, written in faded ink. Who had written these letters, and what secrets did they hold?

Sadie began reading aloud. I think I expected to hear long-lost love letters between Theodore and his wife, but I couldn't have been more wrong.

# Chapter 23

S ADIE WAS IN HISTORIAN heaven.

"Do you realize the significance of these letters?" Her eyes were bright, and her voice was filled with wonder.

As Sadie paged through the collection of letters, she pointed out that most were from Theodore's younger brother, Oakley Stevens.

"Look here," she pointed out. "Oakley used an oak leaf on his letterhead. Cute."

She scanned a few of them, then read some passages aloud. As she proceeded, it became clearer and clearer that Theodore's brother had spent years hounding him for money.

Some requests were polite, even if they were oddly formal. Sadie read one of them in a hushed, quiet voice.

*Dearest Brother. The doldrums of destitution weigh upon me like an anchor of despair. Pray, let thy benevolent hand extend the lifeline of financial succor, so that I may lift myself from the tempestuous seas of adversity.*

She looked up and translated it into plain English. "That means he was broke."

Some letters were angry and accusatory.

*I am convinced that you, dear brother, have pilfered the inheritance that is rightfully mine.*

Some asked for money for his offspring.

*I implore you, dear brother, to cast your gaze upon your nieces and nephews, whose futures are but fragile buds in need of nurturing care. These young souls, your own flesh and blood, have nothing to call their own, no privileges to embrace, and no prospects to ignite the flames of ambition.*

Sadie sifted through the rest of the letters in the box, photographing each one with her phone, then setting them aside.

"I wish we knew how he responded. From the sounds of these letters, it seems like Oakley never thought Theodore did enough for him."

Suddenly the room grew cold. We looked up to see the spectral figure of Theodore Stevens standing before us, his form flickering as it coalesced.

"Can you see him, too?"

Sadie nodded, eyes open wide in surprise. "He looks miserable."

Theodore's voice sounded as though it was coming from far away, like an echo carried on the wind.

"Those letters don't tell the entire story," he sighed. "They were based on a terrible misconception."

He took a seat in a leather wing chair by the fire and slumped his shoulders, looking defeated.

"My brother always believed that I'd been given a great inheritance, and that I'd built my fortune on a secret bequest from our maternal grandfather. No matter how much I tried to explain that I'd started with nothing but determination, he went to his grave believing that he'd been cheated of his share of our family's wealth."

He looked at both of us, his expression sincere.

"I did use an inheritance from our grandfather to start my business, but this was the inheritance." He held out his right hand and pointed to the signet ring on his finger. It was crafted of gold, with a stylized oak leaf on an onyx stone.

"This ring. Not money. Not gold or silver or a secret cache of stocks and bonds. Simply this ring. While it might look like a simple trinket of little monetary value, it was priceless to me. It served as a constant reminder of my grandfather's favorite expression: great oaks from tiny acorns grow."

He smiled sadly. "It was a bit of a family joke, since my mother's family name was Oakes."

He sighed. "There was a time or two when a journalist misquoted me, suggesting that I founded my empire with an inheritance from my grandfather. In point of fact, the inheritance I received was a philosophy, not a financial bequest. I thought that was clear to my relations. Now I know I was mistaken. Looking back at my life now, I regret I didn't make that it more apparent ... and that I wasn't more generous."

With a final, heartfelt sigh, he faded from view.

Sadie and I placed the letters back in the box and returned it to its rightful place within the secret room. We moved slowly, with reverence and respect. Theodore Stevens had revealed the room—and its secrets—and we both felt an obligation to preserve them.

As we closed the secret door, sliding the bookshelf into place, Sadie turned to face me. "Marley, I know this mansion belongs to the Wards, but I feel like this room belongs to history. How long do you think we can keep its contents hidden?"

"I'm not sure. I don't know what the police told them."

Behind us, Hazel stepped quietly into the library. She'd heard us talking.

"I agree," she said. "The Wards have never appreciated the historical value of this home. They'd see dollar signs and nothing more. They'd just strip the room clean and sell everything off without a second thought."

"But don't they know it's here?"

She shrugged. "Mr. Ward simply told me to clean the library, and to make sure there was no sign of Abigail's unsightly death to offend his wife."

Sadie brightened. "It's possible they don't know about the secret room."

"Well, if that's the case, they won't hear it from me."

I took a moment to think, realizing the weight of our responsibility. "Let's see if we can figure out how much the Wards know about the room. We know they haven't seen it yet. Jack and I are the only ones who know how to open the secret door. And if they think Abigail's body was found in the library, they might not come in here at all."

That night, I dreamed that Twila and I were outside, and the little Siamese kitten was playing in a pile of oak leaves. I tried to pick her up, but she kept scampering away, leading me deeper and deeper into a forest of oak trees. Eventually, she stopped and turned to me, carrying a single green oak leaf in her mouth. She dropped it at my side, in a gesture so realistic that I half expected to find an oak leaf on my pillow when I woke up the next morning.

# Chapter 24

T HE NEXT MORNING, I visited Quinn in the county jail. She hadn't been allowed to post bail, and she looked like a shadow of her former self, gray and hopeless in an orange jumpsuit that hung off her slim shoulders.

"They think I'm a flight risk," she explained. "I'm here on a work visa, which means technically there's nothing to keep me from fleeing back to London."

"Is that even an option?"

She chuckled wryly. "No, of course not. My husband is here, my children are here, my entire life is here. Not to mention the fact that I did nothing wrong."

"Do you know what evidence they have?"

"My attorney has asked for full disclosure, but at the moment, it seems strictly circumstantial. There's no trace of the painting or the killers. All they have is the caterwauling claims of those horrible Wards."

"Did they dust for fingerprints? I mean, I'm sure they did. Is that what put you at the scene?"

"I imagine so. It's no secret that I was at the mansion, though. I visited several times in the days leading up to the gala. I toured the entire estate with our event planner as we prepared for the fundraiser. Abigail accompanied us each time, and I had nothing but respect and admiration for that woman."

"Did Calvin Carter go with you, too?"

She laughed ruefully. "Once or twice. What a mistake that was. I included him in the event only because he presented himself as an expert in the field, and he offered to speak for free. On paper, his credentials seemed impressive. Once he got in front of the microphone, though, he made a fool of himself—and me."

I nodded thoughtfully, then broached my next question.

"What do you know about Julian Wainwright?"

"That tall cowboy from Texas? I'd never met him before the gala, but he had been very interested in speaking to me after the event. He came down to the museum the next morning, making inquiries about our Theodore Stevens collection." She fidgeted with the collar of her shirt. "He was enthusiastic, I'll say that much ... but I couldn't tell if he was interested in making a donation or buying our museum outright." She smiled sadly at the memory.

Interesting. While Quinn languished in prison, I couldn't shake the feeling that Julian Wainwright was a far more likely suspect in Abigail's murder.

I took my suspicions to my grandmother so I could get her opinion, too.

The Enchanted Oven was quiet when I walked in. A young mother sipped coffee and nibbled on a brownie while her child napped in his stroller. Two college students swiped and scrolled through images on their cell phones. Gram was in the back, rolling pie crusts, while Kate frosted cupcakes.

Gram came toward the front when she saw me. Smiling, she brushed the flour from her hands. She paused when she glimpsed her reflection in a mirrored pastry case.

"Honestly! Flour in my hair and all over my face. You'd think I was just throwing it in the air back there." She chuckled as she tried to dust some of it off.

"Gram, you're always covered in flour."

"I know, but today ... well, I just want to look my best."

I raised my eyebrows.

She laughed. "Okay. You caught me. Julian Wainwright is probably going to stop in soon, and I don't want him to think I'm always a mess."

I stiffened. "Really? Has he been coming in a lot?"

"Oh, at least once a day," she said, smiling. "I think he might be a bit taken with me."

I bristled. "Be careful, Gram. I think he might have had something to do with Abigail's death."

She shook her head, dismissing the thought outright. "Honestly, Marley. That man couldn't hurt a fly."

I leaned forward and whispered just in case other customers were listening. "Well, there's something a little strange about that guy. Why is he so obsessed with Theodore Stevens?"

Gram pulled a tube of lipstick out of her apron pocket and stroked some on her lips, then dabbed a little on her cheeks, rubbing it in like blush. "I think he identifies with the man. Julian grew up poor himself, like Theodore Stevens, until they struck oil on his ranch. Julian has always loved cowboy hats, so now collecting Stevens memorabilia is just a fun hobby for him."

I scowled warily at her.

"Trust me, Marley. I know he had nothing to do with the missing portrait or poor Abigail's murder."

"If he's as wealthy as you say he is, he could pay to get away with a lot of things."

She poo-poohed the idea. "Nonsense. He's a perfectly nice, normal billionaire."

With that, the bell over the door chimed, and Gram's face lit up. "Well, speak of the devil," she said, smiling. "We were just talking about you, Mr. Wainwright."

He tipped his ten-gallon hat. "I thought my ears were burnin'. Howdy, Miss Montgomery." He grinned at my grandmother, then turned toward me, too. "And a second howdy to you, the other lovely Miss Montgomery."

He ambled over to the counter, his cowboy boots making a soft thump with each step. "If I could get one of those bear claws and a cup of coffee, I'd be most obliged."

Gram used a piece of wax paper to put the pastry on a plate, then poured coffee into a ceramic mug. "You know, Julian, Marley was just telling me she'd like to get to know you better. You both share a certain fascination for history and for Theodore Stevens."

I cringed, but he was too busy admiring my grandmother to notice.

"In that case," he said, "make it two bear claws. My treat."

Gram directed both of us to a table, poured two more cups of coffee, and joined us. She took a sip from her mug and sighed. "I need to sit down more when I'm here," she said. "Sometimes I forget to savor quiet moments like this."

Julian raised his cup to her, and they clinked their mugs in a toast.

"Marley, Julian mentioned something interesting the other day," Gram said, tearing a bite from my bear claw with her fingers and popping it in her mouth. "Did you happen to notice a portrait of Theodore Stevens' mother during the gala?"

"There were a lot of old paintings in the mansion, so no, off the top of my head, I can't say I did."

Julian nodded earnestly. "Well, Miss Montgomery, I spotted it right away. Of course, it helps that I knew what I was looking at. Theodore Stevens' mother, Margaret Stevens, was a right beauty back in her day, what with that red hair of hers."

I took a deep breath. "So what happened to her portrait?"

"I wish I knew. It was there at the start of the night, but I noticed someone had taken it down when I left."

"Where did it go?"

Grandma Clara leaned in conspiratorially.

"That's what we're wondering, too. Maybe the same thief who took the museum's portrait of Theodore Stevens took the portrait of his mother, too. That way, they'd have a matched set."

Julian turned toward her, a gentle look in his eyes. "Let's not be too hasty, Clara. Like I said earlier, there might be a perfectly innocent explanation. With all those people in the mansion, maybe someone just knocked it off the wall, so the Wards took it down until they could rehang it."

"Did you tell Jack about this?"

He cast his eyes up toward the ceiling, thinking. "Now that you mention it, I'm not sure I did. He contacted me for a brief interview, but at the time I was simply shocked to hear that anyone would hurt a hair on that sweet young woman's head."

"Even so," I said. "That's a huge fact to leave out."

"I agree. If I failed to mention it, I should rectify that oversight immediately."

"I'll text Jack to see if he can come over."

Julian smiled. "You tell him there's a bear claw waitin' here with his name on it. My treat."

# Chapter 25

THE POLICE STATION WAS just a block away, so Jack arrived within minutes. He approached our table with a nod.

"Hi, Clara. Hi, Marley. What did you want to see me about?"

Julian stood and extended his hand. "I reckon it's about me, detective. I inadvertently overlooked what could be an important detail about the fundraising gala the other night. These two beautiful ladies were kind enough to call you in so I could correct the record."

Jack motioned for him to take a seat, and I leaned forward so I could hear every word. I also had a few questions of my own, which I couldn't wait to ask. I jumped right in.

"Julian," I said. "Maybe you should start by telling Jack that you carry a .45. Did you have it with you at the gala?"

Julian turned toward me. "Yes, ma'am. I did. I've been carrying a pistol for so long on the ranch that I don't even think about it much anymore. I told the detective about it, too. Rest assured that all the proper permits are in place."

"Did you tell him you're basically obsessed with Theodore Stevens?"

Gram leaned forward, her eyes warning me to slow down. "Honestly, Marley. Manners."

Julian chuckled. "It's no secret that I'm an inveterate collector of anything and everything pertainin' to Mr. Theodore Stevens and his hat company."

Jack glared at me, a silent warning to sit back and let him ask the questions.

"All right, Mr. Wainwright," Jack continued, his tone calm yet firm. "You've shown a strong interest in Theodore Stevens. Can you explain why?"

Julian's eyes lit up, as they did whenever he talked about his idol. "Theodore Stevens was a brilliant artist and a true visionary. I've been fascinated by his work for years. I believe his story is a tale for our times. As an explorer, an inventor, and an entrepreneur, he truly embodied the American dream."

I exchanged an urgent look with Jack, sensing that Julian's infatuation with Stevens was more than just a passing admiration. If you ask me, his obsession was weird. I pressed further.

"Why didn't you tell anyone about the missing portrait of Theodore Stevens' mother?"

Gram glared at me, shaking her head with disapproval. "Marley, I swear, you're bordering on rudeness. Mr. Wainwright is not on trial here. I'd go so far as to say he's not even a suspect." She turned toward Jack. "After all, you've arrested Quinn Delaney for the murder. Isn't that right?"

Jack nodded.

Julian looked earnestly at my grandmother. "Clara, I understand. I have nothing to hide. A beautiful young woman lost her life the other night, and I'll do whatever I can to help the police solve this crime."

I pressed on, turning toward the rancher again.

"Julian, you told my grandmother that you noticed a painting had gone missing during the gala. Why didn't you tell Jack about that?"

"At the time, I didn't appreciate the significance of its disappearance."

Jack held up his hand. "Wait a minute," he said. "Which painting are we talking about? I obviously know about the missing portrait of Theodore Stevens."

Julian's expression turned thoughtful, his fingers drumming on the table. "I noticed a second painting that night that depicted Theodore Steven's mother, Margaret Oakes Stevens."

He stroked his chin as he continued. "It wasn't a prominent piece at the event. I'm not sure anyone but me would have known how important it was. I didn't want to say anything in the moment and steal the museum's thunder, but I was secretly enjoying the fact that I'd seen two Stevens family portraits revealed that night, not just one. Of course, as I left, I couldn't help but notice its absence."

Jack leaned back, processing the information.

"Interesting. Now, Julian, I also have reports you've visited the local historical society and museum, specifically inquiring about Theodore Stevens memorabilia. Can you explain your interest in them?"

Julian flashed a disarming smile, his Texan charm shining through. "Detective, I understand your concerns, but I assure you, my intentions have always been pure. I'm a collector at heart, fascinated by the stories behind these historical keepsakes."

I couldn't shake the feeling that there was more to Julian's interest in Stevens than he let on. I decided to address another concerning observation.

I leaned back, studying Julian intently. "You offered to buy the Stevens Mansion, even though it's not on the market. Care to explain that?"

Julian chuckled, his southern drawl lacing his words. "Well, I can't resist an opportunity when I see one. The Stevens Mansion is a true gem, and I thought it might be a wonderful addition to my collection. It was merely an expression of interest, nothing more."

"You collect mansions?"

"Yes ma'am. I don't like to brag, but ever since a driller hit oil on my ranch, I've had quite a lot of money to invest. I'm 'bout worn out from stocks and bonds and startup companies. Every now and then, I like to put a little money down on my own special interests, like my Theodore Stevens collection. Last year, I bought up his old hat factory in Pittsburgh, and I'm funding its renovation as a historic site. I thought owning his mansion would be a fitting complement to that investment."

Gram shook her head sadly. "You don't need to justify anything, Mr. Wainwright. Honestly, all this talk about money simply isn't polite."

I looked right at her. "Well, neither is murder, but here we are."

No one spoke for a few seconds. Finally, Jack broke the silence.

"Mr. Wainwright, we appreciate your cooperation," he said, his tone measured. "I'll be following up on that portrait of Theodore's mother."

Julian nodded, his confidence unwavering. "Detective, if there's anything else I can assist with, you just give me a holler."

With that, Julian rose from his seat, his charismatic presence filling the room. He extended his hand to Jack, who shook it firmly. Then he turned to me, offering a polite nod.

"Miss Montgomery, it's been a pleasure," Julian said, his eyes twinkling with a hint of mystery. "I hope we can solve this case swiftly and uncover the truth."

I returned his nod, a sense of intrigue lingering in the air. As Julian left the bakery, I couldn't shake the feeling that there was more to his story. Something else was hidden beneath his charming facade.

Jack walked me back to the shop. We crossed the street without a word. He was even diligent about walking me to the corner and waiting for the light, rather than jaywalking.

He looked around to make sure we were alone in the shop. Then he let loose.

"Marley, I know you want to help, but this is still an ongoing criminal investigation. It's not a game. I need you to back off and let me handle it."

I bristled at his tone. "I'm not playing games, Jack. I liked Abigail. I think it's terrible that she was killed, and it's sickening that Quinn is in jail for her murder. I don't think she did it. I know she's not capable of hurting anyone. I just want justice for both of them."

"I understand that, but you can't go around questioning people and snooping around on your own. It's dangerous, and it could compromise the case."

I nodded reluctantly. I knew Jack was right, but it was hard to sit back and do nothing.

"Okay, I'll ease up. I won't do anything dangerous. And if I even catch a whiff of something you should know about, I'll call you right away."

Jack gave me a small smile. "Thanks, Marley." He put his hand on my shoulder, just for a moment. "I'd hate to see you to get hurt."

# Chapter 26

I HAD TOLD JACK I wouldn't do anything dangerous, but that didn't mean I couldn't think about the case.

I decided to review the photos I had taken at the fundraising gala, hoping I'd spot some clue I'd missed before. I pulled out my phone and scrolled through the images.

Most of my photos focused on Gram's baked goods. I had intended to post them on her website and share them on her social media. To supplement the close-ups, I'd also snapped a few pictures of people who were enjoying her creations.

Seeing the images now, in hindsight, was bittersweet. I remembered how it felt to enjoy the excitement of the party, never knowing that a tragedy would unfold before the night was over. It made the whole evening seem far away and long ago.

As I scrolled through the photos, I saw Quinn Delaney and Grace Johnson, one of the museum's guild members. Both were admiring the portrait of Theodore Stevens.

Behind them, I recognized Calvin Carter, the art historian, talking with Abigail. I couldn't help but feel a pang of sadness knowing that this was probably the last photo ever taken of her.

I paused on a photo of Gregory Ward chumming it up with Hawthorne Hill, a reporter from the *Enchanted Springs Weekly*. Gregory had his hand on Hawthorne's shoulder as if they were longtime friends.

I spotted Hillary Ward, a glass of champagne in her hand and a tense smile on her face as she spoke with Julian Wainwright. He had the pocket watch in his hand, and I had the feeling he'd shown it to every single person at the party.

I kept looking for anything that might be useful to Jack and his investigation.

As I continued through the photos, something else caught my eye. In a few of the pictures, a shadowy woman lurked in the background. It was hard to make out any distinguishing features, but I had a sinking feeling that this might be the killer.

I zoomed in, but it was too blurry to make out any details. I sighed in frustration. I couldn't help feeling like I was close to solving the mystery, but the solution continued to elude me.

I needed to get back into the Stevens Mansion, where I could look for answers. Suddenly, I realized I had the perfect excuse to visit Gregory and Hillary Ward—one that would be perfectly safe.

When I called Sadie with my plan to worm our way back into the mansion, she rushed right over. She laughed out loud when she saw the chair I planned to deliver to the Wards.

I'd spotted the chair by a dumpster in the alley earlier that day. Luckily, it was still there when I went to retrieve it for our mission. Its wooden frame, weathered and worn, was held together with mismatched screws, bolts, and gobs of glue. Faded varnish had peeled away, while the backrest sagged in defeat. The spindles leaned in all directions, as if in a perpetual state of rebellion. Three of the legs matched, but the fourth had been salvaged from a completely different chair. No amount of paint, polish, or touch-up magic could hide the fact that time had taken its toll on this peculiar piece.

"It's perfect," Sadie exclaimed. "It's like the emperor's new clothes. We'll tell them it's a valuable antique, and they'll be too proud to admit they don't know the difference. We can even take the truck."

We loaded our priceless treasure of a chair onto the back of the shop's delivery vehicle, a classic red Chevrolet with rounded fenders, chrome accents, and wooden slats around the flatbed. Then we chugged down to the Stevens Mansion. I carried the rickety antique to the front entrance and Sadie rang the doorbell. We heard it chiming inside like the carillon bells of Westminster Abbey.

As we waited, I had another brilliant idea. "Sadie, let's put on those white gloves, so it looks like we're transporting one of the crown jewels." She pulled them from her purse and we slipped them on, trying not to giggle.

After a few long moments, Gregory finally appeared.

"Can I help you?" he asked, his tone guarded. He eyed the two of us with a blank expression on his face.

So he didn't recognize us. That was good.

"Hi. I'm Marley Montgomery, and this is Sadie Arragon. We're from the Enchanted Antique Shop."

He nodded, a vague recollection of the shop dawning on his face. "The thrift store on Main Street?"

"Antique store, actually, but yes. Abigail used to shop with us quite a bit."

You would have thought the mention of her name would have caused some sort of reaction, but he didn't even blink. His expression remained impassive.

"If she owed you money, you'll have a hard time collecting. She's dead."

Whoa. That was cold.

"No," I stammered. "She didn't. I mean, that's not why I'm here. I came to deliver a chair she ordered, before she died." I realized how inane that sounded, so I added, "Obviously. I mean, since she ordered this a few weeks ago."

I gestured toward the wooden chair next to me. If it's possible, it looked even worse for wear after its short ride in the back of the truck, where a few of the nuts and bolts had wiggled loose.

Gregory's brow furrowed, his eyes narrowing as he studied the chair. For a moment, I worried he was wise to our ruse.

"Abigail ordered this chair from your thrift shop?" he asked, his voice tinged with skepticism.

I nodded, maintaining an air of confidence. "Yes, indeed. She was a regular at our *antique* shop." I spoke slowly, hoping he would catch the distinction. "It was a special request—her last request, if you think about it—so I wanted to deliver it personally."

Hillary had joined her husband in the doorway, and she motioned for us to step inside. "Please, come in," she said, her voice filled with a mix of curiosity and sorrow. "Abigail did have a penchant for unique treasures."

Gregory looked skeptical, but he backed up to let us in.

I picked up the chair as if it was made of gold and brought it into the foyer.

I took a deep breath as the weight of the mansion's history enveloped me. The grandeur of the entryway, with its towering ceilings and intricate woodwork, seemed even more impressive now that we were alone in the quiet space. The air was heavy with a sense of mystery and secrets.

I set the chair down, then surveyed the room.

The walls were covered with flocked wallpaper in a traditional pattern of dark green damask on an ivory background. Over the years, sunlight had faded the soft green felt—except for a small rectangular area where artwork had obviously been hanging for years. In that spot, the wallpaper was darker than the rest, like a ghostly shadow of the painting that had once graced the space.

That must have been where the portrait of Theodore Stevens' mother used to hang. I nudged Sadie, and she noticed it, too.

"I see you're in the process of changing out some of your artwork. We have some beautiful oil paintings at the antique shop if you're interested."

Hillary looked at me with a confused expression, and I pointed to the blank spot on the wall.

"Gregory," she exclaimed. "Did you remove that painting?"

"Why would I do something like that?" He walked a few steps closer and scratched his head. "I don't even remember what was there."

"It was that homely red-headed woman with the bland expression on her face. Hardly a masterpiece, but it came with the house."

She exhaled loudly in disgust. "We should report it missing," she said. "I wouldn't put it past that horrible Quinn woman to steal it for her silly museum"

Gregory shook his head. "We don't even know how long it's been gone. Let's ask Hazel before we bring the police around to ask more questions."

"Fine. In the meantime, we've got these two to deal with."

I held my breath as Sadie and I exchanged nervous glances.

As the Wards inspected the chair, Gregory's expression morphed into a perplexed frown, while Hillary's lips furled.

"Abigail ordered this?" she asked, her voice tinged with disbelief.

I nodded, my eyes sparkling with feigned enthusiasm. "I think she intended to display it in the kitchen. It's obviously a primitive artifact, and Abigail said it would serve as a tribute to the ordinary servants who once worked here in the mansion. I could imagine it staged with a set of vintage mixing bowls and a homespun dish towel, for example."

Hillary sighed. "Abigail did have an eye for design, but personally, I don't see this chair fitting in with our décor. I imagine we'll return it."

I had to think on my feet. "Of course, that is one option. We're always happy to accept returns in exchange it for store credit."

"Not cash?"

"Sorry, no."

Hillary sighed. "We do resent having to deal with these situations ourselves. Abigail handled everything. I don't know how we'll ever replace her."

I tucked a loose strand of hair behind my ear. "She was a talented woman."

"I think she might be irreplaceable. Lately it seems like everyone we've tried to hire wants minimum wage. It's like they don't appreciate the honor of employment in a historic home."

Gregory looked sheepish. "Well, there is the one downside to the job."

Hillary tried to shush him. I saw an opportunity, and I took it.

"Is that because the mansion is haunted?"

Hillary recoiled. "Wherever did you hear such a thing?"

Sadie stepped up. "Ever since the gala, people have been talking about the history of the house. A lot of people just assume it's haunted, because of its age and its prominence."

Hillary sniffed. "Well, you tell your rumormongers that there is no basis in reality for such idle gossip."

Suddenly, there was a loud crash from upstairs, followed by a long, otherworldly wail.

# Chapter 27

SADIE AND I CRANED our necks, trying to look up the stairs. "Is there someone else here?"

"No, of course not. Hillary and I were simply enjoying a quiet day here in our beautiful mansion, our home, where we live."

Now there was an even greater wail, followed by the sound of banging and thumping in the upstairs hall.

The Wards looked nervous. Gregory rubbed the back of his neck as if it ached, and Hillary kept glancing over her shoulder as if she was being watched.

"Gregory, we can't hide it from everyone."

I leaned forward. "So there is a ghost."

"Yes. Abigail is the one who told us about her. We thought she was simply repeating old myths and legends, because we saw no sign of her when we first started renovating the mansion. After a few months of remodeling, when we could finally move in, we started seeing and hearing her for ourselves."

"We first saw her in the master bedroom," Hillary began. "Something would wake us in the night, moaning and pacing in front of the windows. It looked like a dark shadow, crossing the room, back and forth."

"We thought it was just our imagination at first, but then we saw her again in the daytime. We'd catch glimpses of her walking up and down the hallway, dressed all in gray, like a grieving widow."

Gregory picked up the story. "We tried to ignore her at first, but then she started throwing things at us. Books, vases, even our precious Hummel figurines."

"The more time went on, the more disruptive she became, until we could hear her crying all night long."

Hillary wiped her nose on a tissue from the side table. "During the day, she was harder to see, but we could hear her, wandering the halls of the mansion, weeping and moaning. It was like she was reliving some sort of tragic event, over and over again."

I sat back, digesting the information.

"It's like she's stuck in a time loop," Gregory said. "Forever searching for something she can never find."

This wraith didn't sound like most of the ghosts I'd encountered, who were simply extensions of their former selves.

"Even Abigail said she was afraid of the ghost," Hillary said. "She believed there was something malevolent about her."

Gregory nodded. "That's why we don't stay here anymore. We retreated to our condo, and Abigail moved out of the servants' quarters and into the apartment over the carriage house."

At that moment, the ghost in question revealed herself. She floated down the stairs, an old woman in a tattered knee-length dress. She was small and withered, with wild gray hair that stood out in all directions as if it had a life of its own. Her face was heavily lined, etched with the marks of grief and anger. Dark trails of black mascara ran down her cheeks, as if she'd been crying for eons. The bright pink lipstick on her lips was smeared, creating a clown-like effect that seemed hauntingly out of place. But what caught my attention were her eyes, filled with a fiery rage that seemed to burn through her very soul.

She reached for a glass paperweight and flung it toward Hillary, aiming straight for her head. I snatched it in midair.

The Wards froze in their tracks, their eyes wide with a mixture of confusion and fear. The ghost circled the hapless couple, wrapping them in a snarl of dark energy that seemed to suck the air out of the room. The message was clear: they were not welcome in the home.

Hillary's voice trembled. "Why does this keep happening?" Her face turned pale and her hands trembled as she clutched his arm. "This is too much. We need to get out of here."

The spirit disappeared in the blink of an eye. Gregory and Hillary wasted no time in making their escape, too.

As they headed for the exit, Sadie and I moved to follow them.

Hillary stopped me. "Wait. The chair."

"What?"

Even in a moment of unfathomable distress, Hillary felt the need to issue edicts and commands. "Don't leave it here. Take it out to the garage, and we'll decide what to do with it later."

I dutifully hoisted the chair up and out the door and we followed the Wards to the carriage house. They climbed into separate cars—a Porsche and a Mercedes-Benz—and shifted them into reverse before either Sadie or I could get our bearings.

"Close the doors when you leave," Gregory called out. "They'll lock automatically."

With that, the Wards sped off, leaving Sadie and me standing alone in the deserted garage.

# Chapter 28

S ADIE AND I LOOKED at each other, dumbfounded, then broke out in laughter at the ridiculousness of it all. Without a doubt, the Wards were some of the rudest people we'd ever met.

"I can't believe they just left us here like that."

"I know. What's the deal with those two, anyway?"

The interior of the carriage house had a certain old-world charm, with sturdy wooden beams and weathered brick walls. The spacious main area had a high ceiling, with plenty of head-room for horse-drawn carriages. There was even a row of wooden stalls along one side of the garage, reminders of a time when horses were more common than cars. Rough-hewn shelves held ephemera from decades of car service, including vintage oil cans, spark plugs, and tire pressure gauges. On a nearby workbench, well-worn tools hinted at the dedicated hands that had once la-bored here.

Sadie tilted her head and studied my face. "Marley, you've got a mischievous gleam in your eye."

I grinned. "Well, technically, the Wards did invite us to come in," I said. "And they didn't tell us when we had to leave."

"What are you thinking, Marley?"

I laughed. "I'm thinking we should look around. This old carriage is just as historic as the main house, you know. Violet told me she knew the driver who used to live here, back when Theodore Stevens had a chauffeur."

Sadie nodded thoughtfully, then smiled. "It's an intriguing prospect. As a scholar, I can hardly say no to expanding my research into local history." She grinned. "In fact, I'm practically obligated to survey the premises."

"The Wards said Abigail lived upstairs. Let's check it out. We might even find some clues the police overlooked."

We climbed a narrow staircase to Abigail's apartment on the second floor.

I expected the living quarters upstairs to be just as rustic as the garage space on the ground level. Imagine my surprise when we opened the door to Abigail's apartment and found ourselves in a spacious, modern apartment. It was a comfortable haven of clean lines and neutral tones. Light flooded in through large windows that overlooked the estate's formal gardens and expansive lawns.

We entered through the living room, where an overstuffed sofa and armchairs had been positioned around a glass coffee table. A large flat-screen television hung on the wall. The kitchen was small but efficient, with stainless steel appliances and marble countertops. A dining table nestled in the far corner, accented with a pillar candle and a small potted plant.

I opened a few cabinets and found nothing but a set of dishes and enameled cookware.

""I assume the police came in to investigate, but nothing looks like it's been touched. Everything's immaculate. I wonder if Hazel cleaned for Abigail, too."

Sadie crossed the room and looked in the fridge. "Well, some- one came in and tossed all the perishables. I suppose the apart- ment will stay vacant until the Wards find Abigail's replacement."

In the bedroom, a king-sized bed dominated the space, dressed in luxurious linens and plump pillows. Abigail's night- stand was sleek and minimalist, with a small bedside lamp, a water carafe, and a brass alarm clock. Across from the bed was a large dresser with a mirror and a bookcase filled with hardcovers. I glanced at the titles. Her tastes were wide-ranging, from *Moby Dick* to *The Art of War* and *The Da Vinci Code*.

The bathroom was the epitome of modern luxury, with a deep soaking tub, a glass-enclosed shower, and gleaming chrome fixtures. Soft towels and high-end toiletries completed the spa-like atmosphere.

The apartment even had a small home office, complete with an elegant writing desk and a stylish leather chair. A few file folders were stacked to one side.

Sadie opened the first file. "Did you know Abigail was re- searching the Stevens family?"

"She never mentioned it when she came into the shop."

"All these records pertain to the Stevens family lineage. Here's a copy of the Stevens family tree. These files are birth, death, and marriage certificates. She's even got old newspaper clippings and census records."

"I wonder if she was doing research for the gala, or if she had some other project in mind." I closed the folder. "She really was devoted to this place."

As we made our way out, I stopped to admire a framed family photo on a side table by the sofa. I could tell it was Abigail, no older than four or five, sitting on her mother's lap. The two shared a remarkable resemblance, with the same sparkling eyes, heart-shaped face, and auburn hair. I wondered if her mother was still alive, and if she would now have the sad duty of burying her daughter.

# Chapter 29

WE HEADED BACK DOWN to the garage, where an old spinning wheel caught my eye. It had been stashed in the corner, apparently forgotten. The piece had to be at least a hundred years old, maybe more, but aside from a thick layer of dust, it seemed to be in perfect condition. It was clearly a valuable antique.

I stepped forward to get a closer look, but I jumped back when I felt the floor move a bit beneath my feet. I hesitated, then tentatively stepped forward again. The floor made a creaking sound, like a rusty old gate.

I took another light step and felt it again, the odd sensation of the floor shifting, accompanied by a groaning sound. It felt like the floorboards in this part of the garage were a different thickness than the rest. When I bent down, I spotted a simple metal ring, tarnished with age and barely visible against the dark wood. I gripped it firmly and gave it a gentle tug, feeling the weight of a trap door lift toward me.

Sadie crowded in close. "First a secret room in the library, and now a trap door in the garage? I guess we shouldn't be surprised. Hidden spaces were common back when the mansion was built."

"The stairs look safe enough," I said, peering down the first few steps. "But I don't see any sort of light switch. Grab that flashlight from the workbench and let's see what's down here."

I thought about calling Jack to report our find, but I knew he would mark it off limits and send me away. I told myself we would just take a quick look, and if we saw anything suspicious, I'd call him.

As we descended the rickety stairs into the dark space beneath the carriage house, my heart pounded with nervous excitement. The musty smell of old wood and dirt filled my nostrils, and the chill of the underground space sent a shiver down my spine.

As we reached the bottom step, my eyes adjusted to the dim light. We were standing in a large storage area. There was an overhead light—a single bare bulb that turned on and off with a pull switch on a string. A few wooden crates were stacked in the corner, and I saw remnants of paper labels that had long since peeled away. A metal handcart leaned against the wall.

Then it hit me. This wasn't just any storage room. This was a smuggler's den. Violet had told me that the Stevens' former driver was a bootlegger during Prohibition. This must have been where he warehoused his illicit inventory.

I smiled to myself. This wasn't the scene of a current crime. We were witnessing the remnants of criminal undertakings from the 1920s. There was no need to call Jack about a crime that occurred more than a century ago.

I softened my gaze, allowing my magical witch vision to pierce through the veil of time so I could see the room as it looked during the Prohibition era.

I normally saw only snippets of the past, but I'd been training myself to expand my abilities. Now, as I stood in the dimly lit underground chamber, I took a deep breath and allowed my senses to attune to the ethereal whispers of years gone by.

As I looked around, a soft golden glow emanated from the ceiling, casting an otherworldly light throughout the room. The air seemed to shimmer with a faint mist.

Slowly, gradually, the chamber transformed before my eyes. The worn stone walls, once plain and weathered, now showed signs of life and activity. Flickering lanterns hung from metal hooks, casting dancing shadows on the rough surfaces. Crates and barrels, stacked haphazardly, housed the clandestine cargo of smuggled spirits, their wooden surfaces weathered and worn by countless secret transactions.

I could hear the distant murmurs and hushed conversations of the bootleggers, echoes of a distant past. Their voices mingled with the thud of wooden crates and the clinking of glass bottles. The scent of aged whiskey and tobacco filled the air, transporting me to a time when the pursuit of forbidden pleasures drove an underground economy.

I turned to Sadie, my voice filled with awe and excitement as I described the scene unfolding before me. "Sadie, it's incredible! I can see how the smugglers hid their alcohol in crates and boxes that filled this entire space."

Just as suddenly, a figure materialized before us, its ethereal form flickering with a haunting light. I knew at a glance that it was Charlie Frankfort, the treacherous smuggler who once called this place home.

His ghostly visage contorted with anger and confusion. He seemed unaware that time had passed, or that he was no longer among the living. To him, Sadie and I were intruders, threats to the sanctity of his ill-gotten gains.

With a bone-chilling howl, Charlie lunged towards us, his withered, claw-like hands reaching for our necks. As Charlie's ghostly figure hurtled forward, his translucent form a menacing blur of ethereal energy, I grabbed Sadie's arm.

In that terrifying moment, something extraordinary happened. As we stared into the face of danger, we forged a telepathic connection that amplified our bond.

As Charlie's ghostly form drew nearer, Sadie's eyes widened in astonishment. Through our heightened connection, she could now perceive what I saw—the spectral visions of the past and the ghostly remnants of Prohibition-era secrets.

Instinctively, she launched into a protective spell.
*Cloak us in a veil of light,*
*Secure and sheltered from the night.*
*In shadows deep, our powers rise,*
*With ancient words and whispered cries.*
*As I chant this sacred rhyme,*
*Guard us now through space and time.*

A shining force field materialized around us, an ethereal barrier of pulsating energy. Just as Charlie lunged, his etheric body crashed into the protective shield. He let out a blood-curdling howl of rage and frustration. His ghostly form disintegrated, dissipating into a swirling, charcoal-gray mist.

The echoes of Charlie's enraged screams reverberated through the underground lair. Eventually, they faded into the stillness of the ancient space.

I looked at her, dumbfounded. "You're not just a spellcaster, Sadie. You're a wordsmith!"

She pretended to dust off her shoulder as if she'd done nothing. Then she laughed. "That was pretty cool, wasn't it? Let's get out of here, though. I don't want to wait around and see what else slithers up through these depths."

We turned toward the rickety staircase. Just as we were about to take the first steps up and away from that desolate old chamber, we heard footsteps pounding on the floor above our heads.

# Chapter 30

I FROZE AS THE heavy footsteps reverberated through the old wooden floor of the carriage house.

"Marley! Marley Montgomery! Are you down there?"

It was Jack Edgewood, and he was furious.

He clamored down the staircase so quickly that if I hadn't known better, I would have sworn he'd jumped through the trapdoor and descended the length of the staircase in a single bound.

He looked at the two of us, his eyes blazing with anger. His fury filled the room, and I couldn't help but feel a tinge of guilt for not calling him when we had discovered the trapdoor.

"Marley!" he bellowed, his voice echoing off the stone walls. "What in the world were you thinking? I explicitly told you to stay away from this case!"

I took a step back, trying to compose myself. "Jack, I—"

He cut me off, his words dripping with frustration. "You've put yourselves in danger, both of you! Do you have any idea how serious this investigation is? You're not detectives. And even though you're witches, you're very young and inexperienced. You don't have the faintest understanding of the dark forces at work in this place."

I swallowed hard, feeling the weight of his disappointment. "How did you know we were here?"

He took a deep breath, a mix of emotions flickering across his face. He let out a sigh, as if contemplating whether to let us know what brought him over in such a hurry. Finally, he spoke, his voice tinged with a hint of sorrow.

"I have a history with this carriage house," he confessed. "I knew the man who haunts it."

We waited quietly, eager to hear more. He continued speaking.

"Back during the 1920s, I was a police officer in Chicago. The whole force was constantly on patrol, looking for bootleggers, trying to stem the tide of illegal hooch. One night, I had the misfortune of running into Charlie Frankfort in a dark alley."

"Our Charlie? I mean, he's not *our* Charlie, exactly, but what was a chauffeur from Enchanted Springs doing all the way up in Chicago?"

"Back then, rum runners had a network that extended from the Windy City to the Florida Keys. Charlie's gang was connected with Al Capone and the Chicago Outfit. I ran into him on one of his trips to meet with the mob."

Jack ran his fingers through his hair.

"I was just a young cop back then, trying to make a name for myself in the mean streets of Chicago. Charlie was slippery, always one step ahead of the law—until the night I cornered him in an abandoned warehouse."

He gazed up at the ceiling, reliving that moment in time.

"As I closed in on Charlie, he knew he was trapped. He pulled out his gun. I pulled out mine. We exchanged fire, and I was hit. I felt the searing pain, and I knew I was a goner. I slipped away, consigned to my fate... but destiny had other plans for me. A passing vampire heard the shots and smelled blood. He saved me."

The revelation was almost too much to comprehend. Jack had faced death and been reborn as a preternatural, all because of Charlie Frankfort. The connection between them ran deeper than I could have ever imagined.

Jack straightened his shoulders and continued.

"So obviously, the story didn't end there. You can't kill a man and get off scot-free—especially if the man you kill becomes an immortal as a result. Ever since that night, I've had a sixth sense about Charlie, about where he is and what he's doing.

"I followed him here to Florida, where he thought he could carry on with his thuggery. I tracked him down, gathering evidence against him, making sure there was no escape this time."

His voice filled with a mix of determination and weariness. "When the law caught up with Charlie, he was handed a life sentence. I made sure of it. He spent the rest of his days behind bars."

"So he died in prison?"

Jack nodded, slowly. "He did. Then he returned to haunt Enchanted Springs. Even with that, he underestimated my determination and the power of a vampire fueled by justice."

Jack continued, his voice heavy with the weight of his past. "I can sense his evil presence, and when I feel him on the prowl, I'm compelled to stop him before he can hurt anyone else."

He took a deep breath.

"For the last few decades, I haven't noticed his spirit moving at all. I assumed he had crossed over to the Dark Side, or wherever old criminals go to burn for eternity. But today, I heard him howling with rage, and I knew he was back to his old habits, in his old haunting grounds. When I sensed his presence here, I rushed over to stop him. I had no idea you two were involved until I arrived."

He paused, looking around the room as if he sensed movement in the underground lair. He held up his hand, motioning for us to step back. His vampire senses had kicked in, alerting him to a presence in the room. As he took a deep breath, his nostrils flared, catching a distinct scent that set his instincts on high alert. Without hesitation, he bounded over to the corner where the old crates were stacked, his movements fueled by supernatural strength.

With a swift motion, Jack knocked the crates aside, revealing a hidden treasure that sent shockwaves through our veins. There, in a heavy gilded frame, was the missing portrait of Theodore Stevens' mother.

But the stunning revelation didn't stop there. Nestled amidst the tangled mess of old straw and debris, a body lay motionless, face down. A jolt of recognition shot through me as I saw the crumpled form, a tall figure dressed in western attire.

It was Julian Wainwright.

# Chapter 31

THERE WAS A SUDDEN drop in temperature as Violet's ghost materialized before us in the underground lair. Her ethereal form shimmered in the dim light, sparkling and glittering as her figure coalesced.

"You wouldn't believe the crack in the continuum we all just felt," she said, facing the three of us. She looked around nervously. "Did Charlie come back? I wouldn't want to see that evil specter for anything in the world, but one of the mansion ghosts told me you were here, and I couldn't let you face him alone."

She glanced toward the back wall, her ghostly gaze falling upon the painting that Jack had uncovered.

"Is that the portrait of Theodore Stevens' mother?" Violet's voice echoed softly, filled with a mix of curiosity and concern. Her translucent figure floated closer to the artwork, her eyes locked on the depiction of the elegant woman.

I nodded, my voice barely above a whisper. "Yes, it is. Jack found it hidden behind the crates, along with ... something else."

Violet's gaze shifted towards the body lying on the ground, and her ethereal features tensed with recognition. "Wait a minute. That's your cowboy friend from Texas. Is he... dead?"

At that moment, the lanky figure on the floor moaned. We all breathed a sigh of relief.

Violet looked at me, confused. "So what happened here?"

Jack called for an ambulance as Julian opened his eyes. "Don't move, Mr. Wainwright. Paramedics are on the way."

I kneeled down and bent over, so Julian could see me without moving his neck. "Do you remember what happened?"

"All I know is that my head hurts like the dickens."

We tried to convince him to stay still, but he struggled to a sitting position looked around. "Wait. I do remember. I happened to be passing by when I saw the garage doors were open. I thought I saw a woman standing in the shadows, calling for help."

"Which woman? Sadie and I were upstairs, but we were the only ones here."

"No, t'weren't you two. Dagnabbit if I can remember anything else, though."

He rubbed the top of his scalp. "I'll be hog-tied if there's not a goose egg there the size of my mama's breadbasket. I'm not even sure my ten-gallon hat will cover it. Where is my hat, by the way?"

I picked it up off the ground and handed it to him. "Dang if the crown didn't get all bashed in, too. Whoever hit me sure did pack a wallop."

He noticed the painting that was leaning against the wall. "Well, lookie there. It's that picture I was telling you about, the portrait of Theodore Stevens' mother. She sure was a purty lil' thing."

The artwork depicted a young woman with fiery red hair cascading down her back in loose waves. She was looking over her shoulder, turned so her face was in a partial profile that revealed her delicate features. Her nose was straight and slender, with a scattering of freckles. Her eyes, framed by thick lashes, were a bright emerald green, with a hint of mischief and intelligence sparkling within them.

Julian rubbed his head. "You might say I got all the sense knocked out of me, but she looks just like the woman who called for help. Of course, it couldn't have been her at all."

Sadie and I exchanged a meaningful glance. Julian was new to Enchanted Springs, but Sadie and I knew that anything was possible here.

The next few moments passed in a blur. Paramedics arrived and took Julian to the hospital. Later I would learn that he had a battery of x-rays, cat scans, and digital imagery, but none of the tests showed any significant injury. Sadie went home, and Violet and I headed back to the shop.

# Chapter 32

RELUCTANTLY, I CONCLUDED THAT I might have been wrong about Julian. I had him pegged as Abigail's killer, but now that he had been attacked too, that didn't seem as likely.

I was at the checkout desk, counting the day's profits on the antique brass cash register, when I heard the bell above the door jingle. I looked up to see Calvin Carter standing in the doorway, looking anxious.

"I'm sorry, Calvin, but we're closed."

"Yeah. I know it's late, but I just had to talk to you."

"Can you come back tomorrow?"

He laughed. "No," he said, his eyes narrowed. "I think I can conclude our business tonight."

He reached into his pocket and pulled out a gun, a snub-nosed revolver that glinted in the moonlight.

"What do you want, Calvin?" I asked, trying to keep my voice steady.

"I want to know what you know," he said, his tone low and dangerous.

"What are you talking about?"

"Don't play games with me, Marley. I know you've been asking questions about the Stevens family. I know you've been investigating. You're a busybody."

"Not really," I protested, even though he was kind of right. "I just seem to find myself in the wrong place at the wrong time. Like now."

He laughed. "Nice try."

I decided the best defense was a good offense. "You're not an art expert, are you, Calvin?"

He laughed wryly. "What gave me away?"

"Everything you said at the gala read like you copied it from an encyclopedia."

He sneered. "So what if I did? No one cared. You think you're so smart, but you have no idea what's at stake here."

He took two steps toward me, waving his gun in the air.

I took two steps back.

"Who are you, Calvin?"

Calvin's face twisted into a cruel sneer. "Does it matter now? You won't be around to tell anyone."

"Just tell me," I demanded.

"All right," Calvin said. "I'll let you in on my secret. I might not be an art expert, but I am the rightful heir to the Stevens fortune."

I gaped at him.

"But Theodore Stevens doesn't have any living descendants."

"He doesn't have any direct descendants—but there were other branches on the family tree." He grinned at me, maniacally. "And since he built his fortune with an inheritance that should have been shared, I'm legally and morally entitled to the wealth he left behind."

I blinked rapidly, trying to make sense of his claim.

"Oh, you are a stupid little girl, aren't you? Don't you see? Theodore Stevens had a brother—my great-great-grandfather."

The pieces clicked. "You're talking about Oakley Stevens."

"Exactly. The world-renowned Theodore Stevens built his wealth by depriving his own flesh and blood of our rightful inheritance."

He glared at me.

"You might think it's too late to care about something like that, but I grew up hearing stories about hidden treasure in the Stevens Mansion. None of us ever thought it was fair that our side of the family had been cut off, especially since Theodore Stevens had used his inheritance to start his hat factory. That money belonged to all of us."

For a moment, he looked wistful. "Imagine how much easier my life would have been if he'd had the decency to share a little of the wealth. Imagine how much different things would have been for me, my parents, my grandparents, if only Theodore Stevens had been less of a tightfisted miser. He stole my inheritance generations before I was born."

Suddenly, it all made sense.

"Back then, did your uncle Oakley ever try to talk to Theodore about it?"

"All the time. He even made several trips down here to this ridiculous backwater village to see him in person. He was rebuffed every time."

So that hadn't been Calvin back at the newsstand. It had been his great-great-great uncle. The genetics in the Oakes family tree were strong.

At that moment, I remembered the family tree on Abigail's desk. I remembered her blue eyes, so similar to her mother's eyes—and Calvin's. I recognized the same red hair, the same cleft in his chin, and most telling of all, the oak-leaf pattern that had popped up repeatedly as I had followed the clues in this case. It was everywhere, on Oakley's letterhead, Theodore's signet ring, Abigail's brooch, and now, in front of me, on Calvin's tie clip.

How had I not made the connection? Theodore Stevens' mother hadn't been born a Stevens. Before she was married, she was an Oakes. I remembered Theodore's words in the secret room. *Great oaks from tiny acorns grow.*

"Abigail was your cousin."

"Unfortunately, yes. When she first took that job at the Stevens Mansion, we had a plan. She would find the secret treasure, and then we'd split it, fifty-fifty. She even came up with a cockamamie tale about the mansion being haunted, so the Wards would leave and she could search unimpeded."

"Did you kill her?"

Calvin's face twisted into a scowl. "I had to. I could tell that she'd found the treasure. She denied it, of course, but I know enough about treacherous relatives to know when I'm being lied to."

He crossed his arms in front of his chest. "She wouldn't let me in the mansion, either. I had to trick my way in, using the fundraiser as an excuse."

"So you killed her."

Calvin's face twisted even more. "Yes, I did. And now I'm the only surviving heir to the Stevens fortune."

He tilted his head back and laughed like a cartoon villain. I'm not making that up. He literally opened his mouth and chortled, "Bwa-ha-ha-ha-ha."

All righty then. Next question. "So why did you steal the painting?"

He grunted in disgust. "Ridiculous! I didn't take it. Why would I want a portrait of that old miser?"

"I'm not talking about the portrait of Theodore Stevens. I'm talking about the portrait of his mother."

"Oh, *that* portrait. Yes, I took it, and I stashed it under the carriage house. What can I say? She was my grandmother. And it's a nice painting ... even if I'm not an art expert."

When he looked back at me, his expression was cold and hard.

"That cowboy tried to sneak in and steal it for himself, but I took care of him."

At that point, I knew our conversation had run its course, and now he intended to kill me.

I raced toward the back of the store. I darted around partitions and displays, using them as cover. The shop was dark, but I knew it well, and I knew where to hide. I saw an old armoire in the corner and ducked behind it, holding my breath and trying to stay as quiet as possible.

I could hear Calvin's footsteps as he searched for me. He was getting closer and closer, and I felt my heart pounding in my chest. I tried to slow my breathing and stay absolutely silent.

As he lumbered through the shop, I heard glass breaking. Calvin must have knocked over a display case in his search for me. I heard him cursing under his breath, and I knew I had to stay hidden.

I crouched behind the armoire for what felt like an eternity. The broken-glass alarm would automatically alert the police. I waited a few more moments, hoping Calvin would figure that out and leave.

I cautiously peered out from behind the armoire. Calvin was still there, scanning the room. Worse, he had seen me.

I had to think fast. Calvin was charging toward me, and I knew I had to defend myself. My heart pounded in my chest as I looked around frantically for something I could use as a weapon.

I spotted an old suit of armor in the corner and dashed over to it. As I approached, I felt a strange energy pulsing through my veins.

Calvin was closing in on me fast, his eyes blazing with fury. "You think you can stop me, little girl?"

I grabbed a mace from the display, a heavy club with an iron shaft.

At that moment, I felt the presence of the knight who once wore the armor. It was as if his spirit had been awakened by my actions, and he was aiding me in my fight against evil. As I lifted the weapon, I felt a surge of power and strength course through me.

I was not alone. I saw him, just for a moment—the knight who once wore this shining armor, his image flickering like a ghostly apparition. He was tall and muscular, with piercing blue eyes and a chiseled jawline.

"You're no damsel in distress," he said. "You're a fellow warrior."

Without waiting for a response, he placed his hand over mine, guiding my grip on the handle of the club. Together, we swung the weapon with incredible force.

The mace connected with Calvin's arm, and he let out a guttural scream. He stumbled backward, clutching his wounded limb.

With renewed strength, I swung the club again and again, until Calvin was down on the ground.

He lay there, moaning softly, not even trying to rise.

The door swung open, followed by the thudding of quick footsteps, and I knew Jack had arrived.

I stepped back, my heart racing as Jack rushed in, gun drawn. "Marley, are you okay?" he asked.

"I'm fine," I said, breathing heavily and using the club to point at Calvin. "But he's not."

# Chapter 33

WITH CALVIN IN JAIL, awaiting trial, most of us quickly settled back into our own routines. Julian Wainwright had been hospitalized overnight for observation. Once he was released, he decided to stay in Enchanted Springs to recuperate fully. "I can't think of any better way to regain my strength," he said, "than to be nursed back to health by Clara's home-cooked meals."

Quinn Delaney was released, too. The portrait of Theodore Stevens was still missing, which distressed her to no end, but its absence had become a major attraction for the museum.

"You've got to see this," she told me when I stopped in to give her the postcards—this time, without being interrupted by an arrest. "People are coming in to see the blank spot on the wall where the portrait is supposed to hang. Everyone seems to think the mystery is just as compelling as the artwork. It's quite the sensation!"

She led me to the display area, where she had hung an empty frame to highlight the place where the artwork should have been. The entire gallery was abuzz with patrons and art enthusiasts discussing theories and as they gazed meaningfully at the blank space on the wall.

Quinn was beaming with delight. "It's the intrigue, Marley! The mystery of the missing portrait has captivated everyone's imagination. Everyone wants to solve the puzzle. It's a real-life whodunnit, and our ticket sales and donations are through the roof."

We couldn't talk long before she was pressed into duty by museum visitors, all of whom had questions about the case. The crowd was mesmerized by Quinn's story, as she described her shock at finding the portrait missing from the mansion. They were even more fascinated by her description of her stint in county jail, serving hard time for a theft she didn't commit.

As I left the museum, she was telling a group of middle-school students how imprisonment had made her stronger, tougher, and more determined than ever to seek justice. "Someone has stolen a piece of our heritage," she said, "and I will do whatever it takes to reclaim that painting for the community of Enchanted Springs."

———

When my friend Ivy stopped by the antique shop to catch up, we settled into the replica of a Victorian parlor that Eleanor and I had created on the first floor.

The space captured the elegance and charm of the late nineteenth century, with patterned wallpaper in deep hues of burgundy and gold. A plush velvet sofa highlighted the center of the display, beneath a sparkling chandelier.

Ivy and I took our seats on a pair of matching tapestry armchairs, with a pedestal table between us. If you didn't know better, you would have sworn we were sipping tea in a British manor house.

I poured Earl Gray from a porcelain tea set with hand-painted floral designs. Nearby, a tall mahogany bookcase displayed a collection of leather-bound books, their gilded spines reflecting the soft glow of the room's Tiffany lamps.

Ivy took a sip of her tea and cleared her throat. "Manny Robinson and I did some digging, and it looks like Gregory and Hillary Ward probably did trick Miranda Stevens into signing over the Stevens family mansion to them."

I raised my eyebrows in surprise.

She took another sip, then peered at me over the top of her teacup. "I remember when the Wards announced they were the new owners of the Stevens Mansion. Honestly, I was more than a little surprised that no one had any inkling of a pending sale."

She laughed. "Okay, I won't lie. I was bitter. I hadn't known the mansion was up for sale, and what real-estate agent wouldn't like a commission on a property like that?" She chuckled wryly at the memory.

"I did some digging," Ivy continued, reaching for one of my grandmother's sugar cookies. "And I found out that the Wards didn't use an agent or an attorney for the acquisition of the mansion. That's a red flag."

I leaned closer, listening intently.

"But that's not even the worst part," she continued. "The power of attorney document they used to transfer the property to their name is incredibly suspicious. For starters, they used a notary who doesn't seem to exist. And the signatures of the witnesses and the notary all look almost identical. It's like they were forged."

My mouth dropped open in shock. "Are you serious?"

"Deadly serious," Ivy replied, her voice low. "If the power of attorney document is invalid, then the transfer of the property is void. Which means the Wards have no legal claim to the mansion, and poor Miranda Stevens was always the rightful owner."

"But what about the money they paid for it?" I asked.

Ivy shook her head. "The Wards paid nothing for it. Somehow, they convinced Miranda Stevens to sign the whole property over to them, free and clear. She probably didn't know what she was signing. After that, she went into a nursing home, where she died within a few months."

"That's wild! So, what does that mean for the Wards?" I asked.

"If the transfer is proven to be fraudulent, which it looks like it is, the Wards could face serious criminal charges."

I felt a knot form in my stomach. The thought of the Wards taking advantage of a vulnerable elderly woman made me sick. "We have to do something. Can we prove the documents are fake?"

"I think we can. Manny Robertson specializes in real estate law, so he's looking into it."

"So what would happen to the mansion?"

"If the Wards are found guilty of fraud, the mansion still belongs to the Stevens family. It's just a matter of whether any heirs can be found."

I sighed. "Well, there's one heir that we know of, but he's probably going to be in prison for years."

As we sat in the parlor, I felt a cool breeze and Theodore Stevens' ghost appeared once again. He looked troubled, and his voice was shaky as he spoke.

"I haven't been seen much since my passing," he began, "because I've been weighed down by guilt. You see, I thought I left my heirs plenty of money to maintain the mansion and live comfortably ever after. But what I failed to tell them was that the money was in the secret room."

Ivy couldn't see him. She was lost in thought, sipping her tea.

"My great-granddaughter Miranda ... she was the victim, not just of the Wards, but of her own family. Her father—my grandson—didn't allow her to marry the man she loved. It destroyed her. She slowly lost her mind, and when her father died, there was no one left to take care of her. She let the mansion crumble around her."

I was stunned into a brief silence as I tried to take in the weight of his words. Finally, I spoke. "But Miranda is gone now. She never had children."

Theodore's ghost shook his head sadly. "But she did have a child. She had a baby daughter with the man she loved. And that child is still very much alive."

I couldn't believe what I was hearing. A secret heiress to the Stevens family fortune? This was beyond anything I could have imagined.

"But how do we find her?" I whispered.

Theodore's ghost smiled faintly. "Don't worry. She's about to find you."

# Chapter 34

A FEW DAYS LATER, Ivy asked me to stop by her office for a special presentation. She'd done more research with Manny Robinson, Sylvia's husband, and they had important news to share.

I loved visiting the old bank building. The facade featured a row of Roman columns and a carved marble pediment. Inside, the original teller windows and walk-in safe were still prominent features in the lobby.

Ivy's receptionist directed us across the marble floor to a meeting room, where a long conference table was surrounded by executive armchairs. One by one, a series of invited guests trickled in. My grandmother Clara came with Julian Wainwright, who looked none the worse for wear. Sadie arrived, beaming with happiness as she talked about the historic bank lobby. Eleanor toddled in, humming softly to herself. Jack Edgewood was accompanied by the chief of police, Notch Arlington.

I was a little surprised to see Hawthorne Hill already seated near the head of the table. If Ivy had invited the reporter from the *Enchanted Springs Weekly*, this was big news indeed. Quinn Delaney took a seat next to him. Gregory and Hillary Ward were the last to arrive, sneering and scowling as they caught sight of our assembled group.

Manny Robinson was next to Ivy at the head of the table, ready with a stack of legal files. The two seats next to him remained empty, with placards that marked each place "reserved."

He opened the meeting. "Thank you all for coming. Ivy and I have discovered some important information regarding the history of the Stevens Mansion, and we thought it would be best to share it with all of you together as a group. We'll start with a very special visitor."

Manny stood as his wife Sylvia entered the room, escorting a weathered old man with fuzzy white hair and wire-rim glasses. She guided him to one of the reserved spots, then sat next to him.

I could tell that she was about to reveal something important. She smiled and squeezed the old man's hand.

"Hello, everyone. I'd like to introduce you to my father, Harvey Washington. He came down from Georgia to share a personal story with y'all."

As her father nodded in greeting, I felt a chill in the air. The ghost of Theodore Stevens materialized, accompanied by the shadowy woman in gray we'd seen attacking the Wards.

Sylvia's father took a deep breath and began to speak in a deep, strong voice that belied his frail appearance.

"Many years ago," he said, "I was a bus driver. It was a respectable, well-paying profession, and I was quite good at my job. I typically drove from Atlanta to Miami at least once a week, with an overnight stopover here in Enchanted Springs."

As he spoke, the ghostly woman in gray began to weep and wring her hands.

"Do any of y'all remember the old Parkside Hotel on the east end of town?"

A few people nodded, including my grandmother, Eleanor, and Jack Edgewood.

Harvey smiled warmly. "That's where I usually stayed during my stopovers, partly because there was a little nightclub there with live music on Friday nights."

Harvey took a deep breath and continued. "During one of those stopovers, I met a pretty young woman in the lounge. At first, we merely said hello to each other, but before long, we got to talking, and we discovered we shared a love of folk music. We enjoyed the same books. We liked the same movies. It felt as though we were made for each other, except for one obvious fact. I was a colored man, and Miss Miranda Stevens was white."

There was stunned silence around the table. Was he saying what I think he was saying?

Sylvia smiled and patted her father's hand.

"Miranda and I fell in love," he said, eyes misty with memory. "Deeply in love. It was a love I never imagined I would feel, and one I've never experienced since."

He looked around the room at all the faces gathered at the table. "We wanted to get married, but Miranda's father wouldn't hear of it. He didn't want his daughter marrying a Black man, and he made that very clear. Miranda was heartbroken, but she couldn't go against her father's wishes."

He shook his head sadly. "It was a different time. Miranda didn't dare stand up to her daddy, no matter how much we loved each other. We continued to see each other—in secret, of course. One thing led to another, and before long, Miranda was with child."

Gregory Ward rolled his eyes and raised his voice. "Where is this story going? I don't understand why we're here."

"Patience," Manny reprimanded him. "You'll want to hear all the details."

The rest of us were entranced. Hawthorne Hill was recording the meeting with his phone and scribbling notes as quickly as he could move his pen across paper. Sadie looked like she was about to implode with excitement. She leaned over to me and whispered, "This is living history!"

"I've been carrying this story with me for much too long," Harvey said. "It's time the truth came out."

Regret was etched on every line of his face. "It was the saddest time of my life. Miranda's father sent her away to a home for unwed mothers and arranged for her child to be placed with an adoptive family."

Then he raised his eyebrows and folded his hands on the table in front of him. "What he never knew, however, was that Miranda arranged for a different kind of placement. She sent the child home with me. I raised our daughter in my family home, in the hills of southeast Georgia, with the help of my own two parents."

As the significance of the moment struck, time seemed to stop.

Harvey looked at his daughter. "Your mother loved you, darlin', but she also knew that it would have been a terribly hard life for you here in Enchanted Springs. Her father was not on her side—or on yours. Frankly, she worried about how you'd be treated if you grew up in that mansion, a little Black girl with a rich, white family."

I felt a lump forming in my throat.

Harvey reached out to hold his daughter's hand. "We didn't want you ever to doubt your value, sweetheart. You were the greatest treasure the good Lord could have given us."

I glanced around the room and saw tears of deep emotion in almost everybody's eyes. Only the Wards looked unmoved.

"At first, we had to keep the baby's placement a secret," he continued. "Miranda and I were afraid that her father would have the child removed from my care. After a year or two, I felt secure enough to send her regular updates about Sylvia's growth, but all those letters came back to me, unopened and marked 'return to sender.'"

In the corner, the woman in gray stopped weeping and stared at Harvey. "He wrote to me? I never received any letters. My father must have intercepted them."

As if he'd heard her spirit speak, Harvey answered. "That's right. They all came back as undeliverable."

Hawthorne, the journalist in the room, asked the questions everyone wondered. "Sylvia, did you know who your mother was? Did you ever get to meet her?"

Sylvia shook her head. "Sadly, no, but at least now I understand why."

Harvey's eyes glistened with emotion. "By the time Sylvia was five or six, I decided it would be best to spare her feelings about her mother's absence from her life. I told her that her mother had died in a terrible automobile accident. I thought that would be easier for Sylvia, never to entertain the thought that she was anything but loved and wanted. Because it's true."

Miranda's ghost nodded her head and whispered, her voice choked with emotion. "It's absolutely true."

Harvey squeezed Sylvia's hand. "Your mother wanted to bring you up herself, but she couldn't. She knew she couldn't. So she made sure you were taken care of as best she could, and then she loved you from afar."

There was a moment of silence as everyone absorbed the weight of the story.

Ivy cleared her throat. "If you'll allow me, I believe I can provide an account of the rest of Miranda's life."

# Chapter 35

WE ALL TURNED TO look at Ivy as she held up an old black-and-white photo of Miranda Stevens. It looked like a high-school graduation photo from the late 1960s or early 1970s. When Harvey saw it, his face softened and he touched his fingertips to the center of his chest, as if he was quieting the beating of his heart.

The black-and-white portrait depicted a young woman with bright eyes and a gentle smile. Her long, straight hair was parted in the center, and she had the cleft in her chin I'd come to expect from all the Stevens family members. I stole a quick glance at Sylvia. I don't know why I hadn't noticed it earlier, but she had a cleft in her chin, too.

Ivy took a deep breath before continuing. "I've spoken with several people who knew Miranda Stevens, and they all described her as a friendly, outgoing young woman who blazed through her school years with drive and determination. After she graduated, however, she became more and more isolated, withdrawing from social events and community life with no explanation."

Eleanor and my grandmother nodded; they were clearly the sources of this information.

Ivy continued. "I think it's clear that losing her child drove Miranda into a deep and lasting depression. Over time, she became a recluse, a shadow of her former self. She simply wandered around the Stevens Mansion, losing track of her money, her time, and her life's purpose."

We were all speechless for a moment, trying to process all the new information. Eleanor looked like she was about to cry. "Poor Miranda," she said. "All those years alone, grieving for her lost love and her lost child. It's just heartbreaking."

Ivy nodded in agreement, sadness clouding her face, too. "Eventually, after Miranda's father died, she let the home fall into disrepair. And then, as she neared the end of her life, she became easy prey to a pair of grifters who took the mansion away from her by fraud. They never paid a cent for that home."

Ivy glared at Gregory and Hillary Ward.

Gregory pounded the table with his fist. "You can't prove any of this. You've seen all the work we've done to refurbish that mansion, and now you're just inventing a story so you can get your grubby hands on what's rightfully ours."

"No," Harvey said. "Every word is true. When I learned Miranda had passed on and her family home was in the hands of strangers, I decided it was time for Sylvia to know the truth about her birthright."

Hawthorne looked up from his notebook. "This is a remarkable story, but how will you prove it?"

Manny Robinson tapped his stack of file folders. "We have documentation that dates back more than fifty years. My father-in-law kept every document relating to Sylvia's arrival on this earth. Believe it or not, Sylvia's original birth certificate lists Harvey as her father, and it's signed in Miranda's own hand."

Harvey nodded. "I also kept every letter Miranda ever wrote to me, and every letter I wrote to her in return." He turned to his daughter with tears in his eyes. "Your mother asked about you all the time. She wanted to know everything about you—how you were doing, what you were learning, and most of all, if you were happy."

Sylvia smiled lovingly at her father. "I was happy. I think I had the most blessed childhood you can imagine."

She turned to the rest of the room. "If you don't mind me saying so, I was raised by a father who adored me and grandparents who worshipped the ground I walked on. My granny even taught me how to cook, which is how I started my catering company."

She chuckled. "If any of y'all have ever wondered where I get my heapin' helpin' of confidence and self-esteem from, it's because of this man here."

Ivy smiled and resumed speaking. "Clearly, the Wards have never been the rightful owners of the mansion. They stole it from Miranda Stevens, which means they stole it from Sylvia, too."

Manny looked directly at the Wards. "I'm letting you know now that we've hired one of the best legal firms in the country, and our attorneys will file paperwork today to reclaim the Stevens Mansion for its rightful heir. We don't expect any lengthy delays. The facts are clear, our evidence is indisputable, and our case is irrefutable."

Jack pulled a legal document from his jacket pocket, too. "This isn't simply a civil case," he said. "You're being charged with multiple felonies, and this is a warrant for your arrest."

The Wards stood, snarling. Gregory lunged for the paperwork in front of Manny, while Hillary lashed out with her fists as she tried to wrench Hawthorne's notebook from his hands. In a flash, Jack and the police chief were on their feet, putting both husband and wife in handcuffs. We watched in stunned silence as the two of them were perp-walked out the door.

Quinn jumped to her feet and raced after them. "Wait!" she exclaimed. "Make them tell you what they did with the painting!"

Back in the meeting room, Theodore Stevens' ghost beamed, the happiest I had ever seen him. And as I watched, transfixed, the gray, bedraggled form of Miranda Stevens underwent a complete transformation. She went from a disheveled old lady with snarled hair and a tattered dress to a beautiful young woman with copper-colored hair and a long white gown that shimmered like a diaphanous veil. She floated over to Harvey Washington and wrapped her arms around his shoulders. He looked up as he sensed her presence. She kissed his cheek, then dissolved.

Julian Wainwright spoke up. "So what does this mean for the Stevens Mansion now?"

"Well," Sylvia said with a smile, "it means that I am moving in—and I have big plans for that place."

# Chapter 36

ONCE AGAIN, I FOUND myself resting peacefully in the warmth and comfort of my bed, in the quiet twilight between dreams and daylight. Soft moonlight filtered through the curtains, casting gentle shadows through my room. I was trying to decide if I needed to flip my pillow to the cool side, or if I simply needed to turn my face toward the open window.

I sighed at the sound of soft footsteps and a faint, playful giggle. If I couldn't pretend to be sound asleep, with no sign of wakefulness, I'd have to respond.

My eyelids fluttered, and the jig was up.

"Good morning, Marley!" Violet Serrano was standing by my bedside, her tiny Siamese kitten nestled in the crook of her arm. She laid the cat at the foot of the bed, then gestured for me to scooch over so she could lie down, too. She rolled over onto her side, her face far too close to mine, watching me with wide blue eyes.

"Wowza," she said. "I might be dead, but I think I can smell your morning breath from way over here on the other side of the veil."

I rolled my eyes and blew right into her face. "Serves you right. It's not like I invited you into my bedroom. What time is it, anyway?"

She lifted her head to look at the clock. "Almost six. Why? Are you going somewhere?"

I groaned.

"Violet, it's so early. Why can't you let me sleep?"

Violet's eyes sparkled with a playful glimmer. "Oh, c'mon, toots. I knew you'd be up. It's sentencing day for the Wards, and everyone's gonna be there."

I smiled, sitting up and stretching my limbs. "You're right. I was almost too excited to sleep last night."

Gregory and Hillary had already been convicted of defrauding Miranda Stevens, and by extension, her daughter Sylvia Robinson. Today they would be sentenced for their other crime—the theft of Theodore Steven's portrait.

Once they had been arrested for their first felony, solving the mystery of the missing painting was almost anti-climactic. The Wards had taken the portrait of Theodore Stevens from their mansion to their seaside condo, then stashed it in a neighbor's storage unit. It was a ridiculously petty move, with an equally ludicrous defense. Gregory said they should be given possession of the work because it had been painted in their mansion. Hillary said they were holding it for collateral until the museum paid their event fee.

Almost everyone I knew was planning to hear the sentencing in person. Quinn Delaney had already called dibs on a front-row seat. Evelyn and my grandmother were going to walk to the courthouse together. Even Julian Wainwright had flown in from Texas for the proceedings. Prison was a given, but everyone wanted to know if the Wards' current terms would be extended for five, ten, or a maximum of fifteen years.

It would be a good day, and an even better evening. After the sentencing, we'd all been invited to the grand opening of Sylvia Robinson's event center. She had transformed the Stevens Mansion into the new headquarters of the Miranda Harvey Company.

Sylvia had hired a full staff of event coordinators, banquet managers, chefs, and servers. She'd upgraded the kitchen with industrial equipment and purchased a full line of banqueting and catering supplies.

She could afford it. When Sadie and I had led her up to the secret room, where Theodore Stevens had hidden millions of dollars in stocks and precious silver, she needed a few minutes to collect herself—but then she went to work, planning and preparing for a bold new future.

With her newfound wealth, Sylvia would be able to expand her business, maintain the mansion, and throw fabulous parties for the rest of her life. She had also founded a training program for hospitality students that her wealth could sustain for generations to come.

In the meantime, she hired Sadie to conduct a full anthropological assessment of every historical artifact in the mansion. The project was turning into one of the crown jewels of her professorial career. With any luck, it could even lead to a tenured position at Magnolia University.

Sylvia had also hired me to take photos for a corporate website and brochure. I'd already taken most of the establishing shots, but tonight I would get photos of real, live people enjoying the mansion—and maybe a few enchanted spirits, too.

I smiled as I got out of bed, more than ready to face the day. My life was calling, and I was in no mood to sleep it away.

# Thank You

Thank you so much for joining Marley on her adventures in Enchanted Springs! For more magical mysteries with a time-travel twist, visit amazon.com/author/ciellekenner. You can also find me online at ciellekenner.com and across social media @ciellekenner.

# About the Author

Cielle Kenner is the mastermind behind the magical cozy mysteries that unfold in the charming small town of Enchanted Springs, Florida—a perfectly normal paranormal community.

Nestled within its borders, time-traveling witches cast spells, spirited ghosts share stories from the great beyond, and vampire detectives take a bite out of crime. It's a place where even the ordinary is extraordinary, and magic merges seamlessly with the mundane.

If the fictional town of Enchanted Springs seems real, that's because it *is* real. The quirky community is based on Cielle's real-life hometown in Central Florida, not far from Ponce de Leon's fabled fountain of youth. It's a place where history is alive and well, which means local legends and lore play a major part in Cielle's work.

When Cielle isn't writing, she enjoys exploring the hidden corners Old Florida, seeking out experiences and locations to inspire new stories. She also has a fondness for cats, crochet, and gently haunted antique shops—all of which find their way into the enchanted world of Enchanted Springs.

www.ingramcontent.com/pod-product-compliance
Lightning Source LLC
Chambersburg PA
CBHW070927250626
47159CB00009B/3155